"Would you care to enter upon a wager with me?"

Lord Stanton's deeply masculine voice intrigued Anne.

"What is the nature of the wager?" she enquired, feeling warm and cozy from the fire and port.

"You believe you can succeed in launching your cousin in London Society and marrying her into the nobility," he said. "I don't think you can succeed and would like to make a wager to that effect."

"What are the stakes?" Anne asked warily.

Lord Stanton did not answer her directly. "I will even the odds by giving you two thousand pounds for your cousin's dowry. However, you may not tell anyone of the dowry until a formal offer is made. The marriage must be to a member of the nobility, and it must take place before the end of July. If you win, I will give you two thousand pounds, as well."

"And if I lose?" asked Anne, feeling dazed by the amount.

"Hell-Born-Harry" looked straight into Anne's eyes. "If you lose," he said slowly, "you will become my mistress for as long as I choose the association to last."

THE IMPRUDENT WAGER

LUCY MUIR

Harlequin Books

TORONTO • NEW YORK • LONDON
AMSTERDAM • PARIS • SYDNEY • HAMBURG
STOCKHOLM • ATHENS • TOKYO • MILAN

Published January 1990

ISBN 0-373-31118-4

Printed in U.S.A.

CHAPTER ONE

ANNE SOUTHWELL OBSERVED the fat snowflakes swirling lazily past the carriage window with a speculative gleam in her green eyes. It was not a particularly heavy snowfall, but it had been increasing steadily since the first flakes had fallen some two hours before.

"How much would you wager we will be unable to make it to the next inn before nightfall?" she asked, turning to her travelling companions. "Give me the chance to win back the shilling I lost to you when it started to snow."

"Oh, Anne, do you really think the roads will become impassable?" asked the worried younger of her two companions, burying her arms deeper in her black fur muff. Her small frame shivered beneath her Witzchoura mantle, and she pulled the fur-edged hood closer about her short black curls. "What will happen to us if we are stranded? I knew we shouldn't travel to London in January. We will freeze to death or starve."

"Don't be idiotish, Melissa," Anne replied somewhat brusquely. "It's unlikely we'll do either, since the snow is barely covering the ground and the carriage has not even slowed."

"Then you shouldn't be frightening your cousin offering foolish wagers," admonished the third occupant of the carriage, a spare grey-haired woman in her early fifties. Her habitually grim expression became even grimmer as she added, "It's not fitting, the way you make wagers on everything. Such betting is for gentlemen, not ladies. Ladies only bet on cards."

"No doubt you are right, Sanders," Anne agreed good-humouredly, smiling at the maid's outspokenness. Sanders was fiercely protective of Melissa, seeming to consider herself a combination lady's maid, governess and dragon aunt. During the year that Melissa and her maid had lived with Anne, Anne had sometimes felt Sanders did not approve of her, but this was the first time she had criticised her so openly. Appreciating the affection for Melissa that prompted the maid's scolding, Anne did not become irritated but made an attempt to explain herself.

"It's a lamentable habit I got into with my brother, Charlie. There didn't seem to be any harm in it between the two of us."

"Between the two of you, perhaps not." Sanders's visage softened slightly at the mention of Anne's brother, killed in Egypt during an early engagement with the French. "But living by yourself in Medford so long you have become unaccustomed to the ways of Society. If you are to chaperone Melissa through a

Season in London you must behave circumspectly or you will cause damage to both your reputations."

"Very well, Sanders, I shall only make wagers with myself," Anne promised placatingly. She smiled at Melissa, who returned the smile with an almost imperceptible shrug, indicating her inability to do anything about her maid's forwardness. Not that she would if she could. Melissa was very fond of her "Sandy," as she called her maid affectionately. Sanders, observing the interchange, sniffed audibly and proceeded to ignore them both.

Anne returned her gaze to the snow continuing to fall outside the carriage window. Her smile faded and a pensive look appeared on her attractive face. The mention of Charlie had brought back memories that seven years of quiet village life had not served to dim. Anne's mother had died of a putrid sore throat when Anne was still a young child, and her father and older brother, Charlie, had raised her in a well-meaning if unorthodox fashion. She had enjoyed more freedom than was seemly, perhaps, and the company of other officers and their families was all she had known. It might not have been a proper upbringing, but she had revelled in it. The day the news of the death of her father and brother in an engagement with the French came, an emptiness had filled her heart. Devastated by the double loss, she had sold their house in Brighton and removed herself to the small village of Medford. She had planned at first to stay only until she overcame the worst of her grief, but time had slipped by and she found herself content to remain in village society.

She had until the past year, that was, when she had unexpectedly found herself the guardian of her seventeen-year-old cousin, Melissa. Her mother and Melissa's mother had been sisters who both married army officers. Anne had met her aunt once when she was a small child, but after the death of her mother the families had not stayed in close contact. Her father told her when her uncle sold out of the army upon succeeding to the baronetcy, and later they received notice of the birth of a child, but they had heard little else. It was something of a shock, then, when a solicitor had informed her of the death of her aunt and uncle in a curricle accident, and told her she was the guardian of a cousin she had never met.

Anne had instructed Melissa to come live with her in Medford, planning to take her to Bath or Brighton for a modest come-out when the year of mourning was up. Her first view of Melissa had destroyed such plans, however. Her cousin proved to be an enchantingly lovely young woman, and Anne knew she would not be doing her justice to present her anywhere but London. She must be given the chance to make the good match to which her beauty and sweet nature entitled her. Accordingly, Anne made plans to take her to London for the Season. The local squire's wife, a close friend of Anne's, had been most helpful, even loaning her carriage and coachman for the journey. Anne knew that it would not be easy to launch Melissa in London Society, even with her beauty. Hence the journey to London in January so they could have time to become established before the Season began in April.

Anne glanced at her cousin, who had fallen asleep against the worn green velvet upholstery of the carriage, marvelling anew at her beauty. Glossy black curls peeped from under the fur trim of Melissa's hood, framing a perfectly oval face with finely moulded features. Long black lashes fanned over her rosy cheeks, concealing a pair of forget-me-not blue eyes. So different from her own average blonde prettiness, Anne thought wistfully. She sighed softly and, turning once again to the carriage window, began to amuse herself by betting which snowflakes would melt and trickle to the base of the window first. She was down about two guineas when she was forced to halt her betting as the snow became so thick and heavy it was impossible to distinguish individual snowflakes upon the window. She noted that the carriage had begun to slow and was not surprised when, in a short time, it ground completely to a halt.

"What is it?" Melissa cried in surprise, waking.

"The carriage appears to be stuck. Perhaps I'll win my wager after all," Anne replied, ignoring Sanders's disapproving look. It was to be her last wager, after all.

The carriage door opened, letting in a swirl of snowflakes, and the cold-reddened face of the coachman appeared.

"It's no good, miss. Carriage is stuck fast in a snowdrift."

"How far do you think we are from the next inn?" Anne queried.

"Six miles, or thereabouts. Too far to walk, miss. But we passed a road to what appeared to be an estate a short while back. I could go there and ask for shelter."

"Do you have any idea whose estate it is?"

"No, miss."

"It doesn't appear we have any other choice. We'll wait here until you return. I doubt there will be any other vehicles on the road."

"I'll leave Jem groom with you and be back as soon as I can, miss."

The coachman closed the carriage door, shutting in the cold air. Anne addressed Melissa, who was now shivering in earnest.

"The estate owner may not be in residence, but there should at least be caretakers who will give us shelter. What odds..." Anne trailed off. She *would* have to guard her tongue. She had been about to bet whether the owner was in residence and what his rank might be.

"I just hope the coachman returns quickly," Melissa said. "It's getting so cold."

Anne observed Melissa's white face and chattering teeth with concern. Sanders, her expression grim as usual, tucked the plaid carriage blanket closely about Melissa, tugging it clear up to her chin. Melissa hugged herself beneath it, trying to get warm, and the three waited in silence for the coachman's return as the storm worsened. Anne pulled her plain brown travelling cloak more tightly about her, and thought of Jem waiting outside. She hoped he was warmly dressed.

Although it seemed longer, less than an hour had passed before the carriage door swung open and the coachman appeared once again.

"We're in luck, miss. The owner's in residence and I've brought help," he said briefly.

He slammed the door shut and the three passengers had a glimpse of four strong-looking bays being led past the carriage. The carriage rocked uncomfortably as their exhausted horses were unharnessed and the bays hitched to it. Then, with a sudden lurch, the fresh horses pulled them free from the drift. The coachman expertly turned the carriage around, and they headed back in the direction they had come.

In a short time they turned off the main road, and Anne had a glimpse of two large gate piers, indicating the presence of an estate. As they passed through the gates and down the drive, Anne tried to see the estate grounds, but the snow was falling so heavily that she could not make out anything beyond the edge of the road. She wondered who the owner was. Melissa remained silent, too cold to be interested in the estate or to speculate on its owner.

Anne had little time for conjecture herself. The fresh horses pulled the carriage through the snow easily, and it wasn't long before they halted before a large dwelling. A snow-covered Jem opened the carriage door and let down the steps while the three passengers prepared to get out. After Jem assisted her from the carriage, Anne stood a moment looking at the house while she waited for Melissa and Sanders. The outlines of the building were obscured by gusting snow, but she was able to determine that it was a very large severe structure of grey stone. As soon as she alighted from the carriage, Melissa hurried up the short flight of steps to the entrance with Sanders. Anne followed more slowly.

The doors swung open at their approach, and the three stepped into the welcome dryness and warmth of a great entrance hall. Their wraps were taken by a footman, and Anne had a confused impression of an interior opulence at odds with the severe exterior of the house before her attention was commanded by a dignified man of middle years.

"Welcome to Longworth, Miss Amberly, Miss Southwell," he said, evidently having been informed of their identity. "I am Upton, Lord Stanton's butler, and this is Mrs. Tompkins, the housekeeper," he added, indicating a matronly woman beside him.

Mrs. Tompkins took one look at Melissa, still shivering, and exclaimed, "The young lady looks frozen to death! We must get her into a warm bath at once."

She took charge of Melissa and Sanders, disappearing down the black-and-white marble hall with them, leaving Anne alone with Upton.

"This way, miss," Upton said to Anne, unsure whether the woman he was left with was Miss Amberly or Miss Southwell. "If you will wait in the Red Drawing Room, his lordship will join you shortly."

Longworth...Lord Stanton... Anne mused as the butler ushered her into a large drawing room on the ground floor and left her alone. Where had she heard those names before? They were vaguely familiar, but she couldn't quite place them. He was obviously very wealthy, she decided as she looked about the room, noting the richness of the furnishings. Heavy velvet draperies dimmed the light from the windows, and ornately carved and gilded chairs and sofas upholstered in red velvet ranged around a textured Savonnerie carpet of red and black. The walls and ceilings were heavily ornamented with sculpted gilt decorations, and several large paintings in elaborate frames hung on the walls. It was very different from the lighter style now in favour, but Anne decided she liked it. Despite its opulence, the room was somehow inviting.

She was drawn to the fire blazing in a white marble fireplace across the room and went to bend over it, holding her icy hands close to the roaring flames. Her hands warmed quickly, and as she straightened, her attention was caught by the painting above the fireplace. It was certainly an odd choice for its central position in a formal reception room, she thought. While it was an undeniably beautiful painting, conveying light and motion, it was also undeniably erotic. The graceful nude female forms tumbling over one another in the brightly coloured sylvan setting seemed to invite onlookers to join them. Anne wondered who the artist was, deciding to put her money on Rubens. As she searched for a signature to verify her guess, a voice came from the doorway behind her, seeming to answer her unspoken question.

"I see you are admiring my Fragonard."

CHAPTER TWO

"ACTUALLY, I WAS JUST BETTING with myself that it was a Rubens," Anne replied, turning around. "I see I would have lost my guinea."

Her tongue stilled as she saw the incredibly handsome man standing in the doorway. He looked to be just under six feet tall, and his slender yet athletic physique showed off to advantage his close-fitting blue superfine coat and pantaloons of ribbed kerseymere. The soft frills of his shirt fell above a buff waistcoat, and a pristinely white neckcloth contrasted sharply with his dark complexion and black hair. He smiled at Anne and walked leisurely towards her.

"One should never make wagers on things of which one has insufficient knowledge. If you will notice, the figures are less robust and the background less distinct than in a Rubens." He made a graceful bow as he came up to her. "Henry Stanton, Marquess of Talford. Do I have the pleasure of addressing Miss Amberly or Miss Southwell?"

"My lord." She curtseyed, trying again to place the familiar-sounding name, "I am Anne Southwell. Thank you for giving us shelter here."

"It is a pleasure to be of assistance. I am glad I decided to remain at Longworth after the Christmas festivities."

Very glad, he thought to himself, frankly admiring the woman before him. Even the outmoded brown merino dress she wore could not conceal her beauty. She was something below middle height, but held herself with an erect yet easy posture that made her seem taller. He appreciated her regular features and candid green eyes, but it was her heavy honey-blonde hair dressed in classical coils that his glance stayed on longest. He had a sudden desire to see that hair loose and flowing over her shoulders and back.

Anne felt a warmth that had nothing to do with the heat of the fire at the marquess' frank appraisal of her person. Up close, the marquess was even more disconcertingly handsome, although silver glints in the black hair casually arranged *à la* Titus indicated he was older than she had first thought. A memory suddenly clicked into place. Lord Henry Stanton, "Hellborn Harry." Of course! Her brother had often admiringly recounted the escapades of the famous rake. He was a member of the Prince's set and had been infamous for his duels, deep gaming, and the many dashing high-flyers with whom he had been associated. The more respectable members of the ton had predicted that he would come to a bad end, but instead he had increased his already considerable wealth.

Lord Stanton saw the gleam of recognition in her eyes and said with amusement, "I see you have heard of me, Miss Southwell. No doubt you are wishing yourself still safe in your carriage. Death by freezing would be preferable to being snowbound in Hell-born Harry's home."

Perhaps she *should* think that, thought Anne, but instead she felt intrigued. After all, this was her first meeting with a real rake. Charlie's rackety friends had not merited such a distinction.

"Indeed not, Lord Stanton. I am not so missish to prefer frostbite to the warmth of a fire simply because that fire is in your home. Although perhaps I should be concerned on behalf of my cousin," she added.

"Let me set your mind at ease, Miss Southwell. I have been informed that your cousin is quite young, and I have no taste for cradle robbing, no matter how beautiful the occupant of the cradle."

"I wager you may change your mind after you see her," Anne said, not believing any man could remain immune to her cousin's beauty.

"You would lose again," Lord Stanton replied. "My taste runs to more mature women," he added, looking at her meaningfully.

Lord Stanton found himself becoming even more attracted to this woman by her common-sense acceptance of a situation that would have sent most gently reared ladies into a fit of vapours or spasms. He smiled at her again and she returned the smile spontaneously.

A footman entered and set a tray with two glasses and a decanter on a table. Lord Stanton poured a small measure into one glass and offered it to Anne.

"Brandy, Miss Southwell? It will help to stave off a chill."

Anne hesitated a moment before accepting the strong spirits, then decided her ordeal in the storm made it acceptable to have some. Their fingers touched slightly as she took the glass, causing a tingle to run from her fingertips up to her spine. She sensed the touch had been intentional, although perhaps she was unfairly judging him because of his reputation.

"Please be seated if you have warmed yourself sufficiently, and tell me how you came to be travelling in such inclement January weather," he said. "Miss Amberly and your servants have been attended to, so you need not concern yourself on their account."

Anne sat down in a red velvet chair near the fireplace and Lord Stanton seated himself across from her, his legs stretched out casually, booted feet crossed. Anne found that his relaxed attitude put her at ease, as well. The brandy was already taking effect, warming her insides and making her receptive to his charm. Before long she was freely relating to him something of her life in Bath as the motherless daughter of an army officer. A small voice in her mind cautioned that she was telling too much to a relative stranger, and a rake at that, but Anne ignored the voice. The brandy had loosened her tongue, and she discovered that she was starved for masculine company—someone to listen to her and give advice the way Charlie had.

A wistful look came over her face at the thought of Charlie, and she stopped speaking a moment, remembering her devil-may-care brother. He hadn't looked anything like Lord Stanton—Charlie had been of very slender build, with merry hazel eyes and wavy golden hair—but they both had the same indefinable masculine charm.

Lord Stanton noticed the change in Anne's expression and prodded softly.

"What are you thinking of, Miss Southwell?"

"I was just thinking of Charlie," she replied, her eyes losing their unfocussed look and meeting her companion's.

"Your brother?" Lord Stanton inquired, referring to an earlier part of their conversation. "You must have been very close. He was of an age with you?"

"No," Anne said, her glance slipping past Lord Stanton's again and staring beyond him into the past, "he was older than I. Charlie helped Papa raise me after my mother died."

A smile touched Anne's lips and she laughed softly. "I daresay some of the things Charlie thought it necessary to teach me were not quite proper for a young girl, but he and Papa never made many allowances for my being female."

She took another swallow of brandy and savoured the warmth it engendered in her body and mind. It made it easy to talk with Lord Stanton about her brother.

"One time," she said reminiscently, "I came upon Charlie and two of his friends betting which of two garden toads would catch a bug first. I insisted that I be allowed to make a wager too, and lost a guinea to them. Only I didn't have a guinea.

"Charlie was quite horrified that I had made a wager for which I did not have the stakes. After his friends left he told me that I had quite shamed him, and that I must come up with the money to settle my debt. The only thing I could think of was to give him my garnet necklace to pawn, which he did.

"About a week later, our housekeeper was helping me dress for a dinner at Colonel Morehead's and asked me where the necklace was. She was quite shocked when I confessed what I had done with it and went to inform Papa. He sent for me and told me to repeat the story. He looked very stern, and I was afraid both Charlie and I were going to be severely punished, but after he heard me out he told the housekeeper that Charlie had done the right thing to teach me that even a woman always paid her debts of honour."

Anne fell silent again, and her expression sobered. "Charlie was always so full of life." She shook her head slowly. "I could not believe it when I was informed both he and my father had been killed in the action in Egypt."

To her horror, Anne felt tears forming in her eyes and blinked furiously to prevent them from falling. It was not the thing to burden another with one's personal sorrows.

Lord Stanton said nothing but looked at her sympathetically and allowed her time to regain control of her emotions.

"But that was seven years ago," she said, regaining her composure. "I sold our house and moved to Medford. I lived there quite contentedly until I found myself Melissa's guardian."

Her moment of melancholy over, she went on to tell Lord Stanton of her ward's circumstances and how her beauty and sweetness had moved Anne to change her plans to present her in Bath and try instead to launch her into London Society.

Lord Stanton listened with attention to Anne's tale, careful to let his dark eyes betray nothing of his thoughts. He had been suffering from ennui, and here was a heaven-sent opportunity to relieve it. He took careful note of Anne's words, storing the information away. Daughter of an army officer, well past the age of consent, with an unorthodox upbringing. Good—her background and age made this lovely woman before him fair game. His considerable experience told him the attraction was mutual, and he contemplated an enjoyable pursuit. She was certainly naive about Society, however, to imagine that she could marry an impoverished ward into the nobility, no matter how beautiful the girl might be.

"My dear girl," he said as Anne finished her recital and lapsed into silence, "you have set yourself an impossible task."

"Why? I realise it will be difficult. That is why we are on our way to London now. I shall have time to reconnoiter and plan my campaign before the Season begins in April."

"Spoken like the true daughter of Major Southwell." Lord Stanton smiled and took another sip of brandy. "But it is obvious you have no acquaintance with London Society. Neither you nor your cousin has a fortune or a title. No matter how beautiful your cousin is, you would at least need to have a well-placed relative or friend to sponsor you into the ton, and if I understand you correctly, you have neither. You are not even travelling with a proper companion. You may be past one-and-twenty, but you are unmarried and therefore not an acceptable chaperone. Take my advice and introduce your cousin into Bath society as you originally intended. There you would have some chance of succeeding."

During his speech Anne found her previous good opinion of Lord Stanton dissipating. He was being like

Charlie in his less endearing moments—condescending to her and finding fault with her plans. She put her brandy glass down on the table beside her and sat up straight.

"I am nine-and-twenty, Lord Stanton, far old enough to serve as a chaperone to an eighteen-year-old girl, whether I have been married or not. Thank you for your kind advice, but I feel I would not be doing justice to Melissa were I to marry her off to some elderly noble in Bath. I will continue to London."

"Then I wish you every success in your endeavour," Lord Stanton replied mildly.

Anne relaxed her hostile posture, and he smiled at her again, pleased to see his smile returned. She had spirit as well as beauty. Better and better. A plan began to take shape in his mind, but it was too early to put it into operation. He rose and tugged a bellpull.

"I know you would like to see how Miss Amberly fares and to have the opportunity to rest before dinner," he said to her. "Gates will escort you to your rooms. Dinner has been set back to eight o'clock. Until then..." He bowed over Anne's hand as she rose to leave the room.

HENRY STANTON WATCHED ANNE follow the footman from the room with a half smile on his lips. Yes, he was very glad he had chosen to remain behind at Longworth after his holiday guests had gone on to

Headley Hall for more festivities. He poured himself another brandy and returned to his seat before the fire.

At forty years of age, Lord Henry Stanton was one of the few members of his set who remained unmarried. Not that marriage slowed the others down in their pursuit of pleasure. But Harry had no desire to encumber himself with a wife, no matter how compliant she might be. Each Season he watched cynically to see which mamas would allow the draw of his title and money to overcome their repugnance of his reputation and throw their daughters in his way. He carefully gave them a wide berth and confined his pleasures to married women and women of the demimonde.

He contemplated Miss Southwell with a stirring of desire. She was the kind of woman he found most appealing—attractive, intelligent and old enough to have formed opinions of her own. The fact that she had been brought up by a father and brother who were army officers would be to his advantage. They had evidently exposed Anne to more of life than was usual for a gently bred woman. Still, he would have to go carefully in his plans to seduce her. She was obviously untouched despite her upbringing. He wondered why she had never married. Probably she had lacked suitors of acceptable age and status in Medford. He briefly debated the ethics of what he planned to do, but again came to the decision that her age and station in life made her fair game. Or else he was making excuses so he could seduce the most desirable woman he had come across in years with a clear conscience, he recognized cynically. Well, no woman had ever lost through an association with him. He was unaccustomed to denying himself anything he wanted, but he also prided himself on his considerate treatment of his mistresses. It was fortunate that his sister had not come to Longworth for the holidays. Her presence would have made his plans impossible.

He shifted in his chair at the thought of his sister, Lady Caroline Brookfield. Although she never presumed to lecture him, he knew she never gave up hope that he would settle down and abandon his rakehell ways. Perhaps someday, he mused, when he had three score years to his credit and wanted someone to care for him in his old age. But now there were still too many pleasures to be had, such as Anne Southwell.

GATES SHOWED ANNE into a bedchamber on the next floor where she found a young girl unpacking her clothes. The girl stopped her work at Anne's entrance and curtseyed.

"I'm Mary, miss, and I'm to be your maid while you're here, if you wish it."

"Thank you, Mary," Anne replied, looking about the room with interest. The walls were covered in paper painted with delicate flowers and leaves in soft hues. A bed with peach-coloured tent-style hangings was against one wall, and two patterned carpets of silk graced the floor. A small writing desk was placed conveniently, a wash table in the corner, and several chairs upholstered in peach damask were set about the room.

"What a beautiful room this is," she said appreciatively.

"Isn't it, miss," Mary answered shyly. "It's called the Chinese Bedchamber, miss."

Anne removed the worst of her travel stains at the delicate toilet table, and Mary helped her into a burgundy gown suitable for dinner. Anne surveyed herself critically in the gilt-framed glass, frowning slightly. She must get some new gowns when she got to London. Hers were sadly out of fashion. Well, it would have to do, she decided, pinning a half handkerchief on her head as befitted her age and unmarried status.

Mary showed Anne into a bedchamber directly across the hall where she found Melissa sitting up in a gilded bed with blue-and-white curtains. Sanders was folding clothes into a large wardrobe.

"Where have you been so long, Anne?" questioned Melissa eagerly. "Have you met Lord Stanton yet? What is he like?"

Anne seated herself on the bed next to Melissa, anxious to impart her news.

"Yes, I met him. That's what detained me so long. You'll never guess who he is—'Hell-born Harry'!

Charlie used to tell me stories about him. He thought he was quite a nonpareil."

"Hell-born Harry? Who's that?" Melissa asked.

Sanders halted her work and interrupted their conversation. "Ha! I feared as much when Mr. Upton first told us his name. We had best leave as soon as possible. Should it become known you stayed here your reputations would be quite ruined."

"Fustian, Sanders," Anne said heatedly, her brief pique at Lord Stanton's discouragement of her plan over. "He behaved in a most gentlemanly manner. And I am here to chaperone Melissa."

"Who is here to chaperone you, miss?" Sanders asked shrewdly. She sniffed pointedly. "Drinking brandy alone with a rake is not the thing for a gently bred lady."

"A rake? Who *is* Hell-born Harry?" Melissa repeated.

"It's not fitting you should know about him, a young girl not yet out," Sanders said. "It's enough for you to know that he should not be encouraged in any way by either of you. Although," she added fairly, "he seems to have mellowed somewhat in the past several years."

A new thought occurred to Anne, a strangely unwelcome one. "Is he married?" she asked Sanders.

"Married? That one?" snorted Sanders. "What need has he to marry? Besides, no properly brought up young lady would have him."

"Well, I think his reputation is grossly exaggerated. What would you wager..." Anne's voice trailed off. She looked sheepishly at Sanders and hurriedly changed the subject. "Melissa, do you feel recovered enough to go down to dinner?"

"Yes. The warm bath and short rest revived me completely. I wouldn't miss meeting Lord Stanton."

ANNE TOOK ANOTHER BITE of the tasty haricoed mutton, enjoying the best prepared meal she had had in ages. Lord Stanton evidently employed a very good cook. She looked at Melissa to see if she were enjoying the meal and was amused by the expression of disappointment evident on her face. Anne knew it did not reflect upon the food but on Lord Stanton. She had been most diverted to see the expression of apprehension on Melissa's face when she first met Lord Stanton quickly change to one of chagrin when he displayed no signs of rakishness but behaved quite as any other gentleman of her acquaintance.

Lord Stanton caught her eye and smiled, and Anne knew he was sharing her amusement. Not for the first time during dinner she wished she had on a more fashionable gown than her plain cambric round gown. She felt out of place. Lord Stanton was impeccably clad in a claret coat with a quilted white marcella waistcoat and kerseymere breeches, and Melissa looked very modish in a tunic of printed rose muslin over an underdress of white muslin.

Surprisingly, though, Lord Stanton had not appeared to be overcome by Melissa's beauty when he was introduced to her. Indeed, Anne felt that he was unaccountably drawn more to her. She glanced at Lord Stanton again and once more found his eyes upon her. She had an uncomfortable feeling that every time she looked his way he was aware of her regard. She felt herself blush and looked down, concentrating her attention on the mutton and the beautiful Derby tableware.

Lord Stanton saw the light flush staining Anne's cheeks and knew her awareness of him was a good sign. She was looking absurdly young in her simple burgundy round gown and the half handkerchief pinned over her magnificent hair. Miss Amberly was as beautiful as Anne had indicated, but he appreciated her beauty without being drawn to it. He preferred fair women.

A question from Melissa recalled him to his duties as host, and he turned his attention to her. For the rest of the meal he exerted himself to amuse both his guests with stories of Town and Court.

Since there were no other guests present, Lord Stanton did not sit in solitary state with his port after dinner but chose to join Anne and Melissa in the drawing room that adjoined the dining room. It was smaller than the red drawing room Anne had been in earlier, but as opulently furnished and decorated in shades of yellow and green. Anne quickly looked at the paintings lining the walls but saw none similar to the Fragonard in the red drawing room.

"I do own more Fragonards, Miss Southwell, but they are hung in other rooms," said Lord Stanton, correctly interpreting Anne's searching look.

Anne blushed again, and taking pity, Lord Stanton changed the subject, motioning to a beautifully cased chamber organ at one end of the room.

"Do either of you play?"

"I am only conversant with the pianoforte, but Anne plays very well," volunteered Melissa.

"Please honour us with a selection, Miss Southwell," he requested.

Anne agreed and, seating herself at the small organ, began a piece by Handel. Lord Stanton and Melissa sat quietly, enjoying the skill Anne displayed in her performance. When she finished the piece, Melissa rose and begged to be excused, pleading fatigue after the long day of travel. She waited for Anne to accompany her, but Lord Stanton intervened, asking Anne to play another selection for him. Anne acceded gracefully, and after bidding Melissa good-night, she reseated herself at the organ and played a short composition by Bach.

"Thank you, Miss Southwell," Lord Stanton said when she had finished. "You play beautifully."

"It is one of the few accomplishments I managed to acquire," Anne said, smiling. "My father did not concern himself with seeing that I received instruction in womanly accomplishments. However, we had a chamber organ that had belonged to my mother, and I begged to learn to play it."

She got up from the organ and crossed the room to Lord Stanton, who rose at her approach.

"Please excuse me now, Lord Stanton. It has been a tiring day."

"Stay a moment, Miss Southwell," Lord Stanton requested. He indicated a chair to her and rang for a servant. "Please join me in a glass of port before you retire. It will make you rest more easily."

Anne hesitated a moment, remembering Sanders's warning. She sensed Lord Stanton was attracted to her, and he *was* Hell-born Harry, after all. Then she scolded herself for being missish and sat down on the gold-and-yellow brocade chair he had indicated. Lord Stanton took the port from Upton when he entered, offered a glass to Anne and seated himself across from her. For a few minutes they sat in companionable silence. The window draperies had not been drawn, and a full moon illuminated a silvery frozen landscape. The contrast of the cold outside and the warmth she was sharing inside with Lord Stanton created a feeling of cozy intimacy. She thought again how she missed masculine company and relaxed into her chair, enjoying his presence.

At length Lord Stanton broke the silence. "When I first met you this afternoon you were making a wager with yourself," he stated, smiling at her but not shifting from his comfortable position. "Would you care to enter upon a wager with me?"

"What is the nature of the wager?" Anne inquired, surprised, waking from a half sleep induced by the warmth of the fire and the port.

"You believe that you can succeed in launching your cousin into London Society and marrying her into the nobility. I don't think you can succeed and would like to make a wager to that effect."

"What are the stakes?" Anne asked warily, remembering how her brother, Charlie, had often tried to trick her into impossible wagers. Lord Stanton had the same look of mischief in his eyes.

Lord Stanton did not answer her directly. "I will even the odds by giving you two thousand pounds for your cousin's dowry. This would allow you to use what monies you have to make a better appearance. However, you may not tell anyone of the dowry until a formal offer is made. The marriage must be to a member of the nobility, and it must take place before the end of July. If you win, I will give you two thousand pounds, as well."

"And if I lose?" asked Anne, feeling dazed by the amount. Two thousand pounds! That was more than the total she and Melissa had for the Season combined.

Lord Stanton looked straight into Anne's eyes. "If you lose," he said slowly, "you will become my mistress for as long as I choose the association to last."

CHAPTER THREE

SILENCE AGAIN FILLED the drawing room, but it was a taut silence, not the companionable kind of a few minutes before. A sense of unreality settled over Anne. She heard the ticking of the ormolu clock on the mantelpiece, the snapping of the burning logs and saw Lord Stanton's half smile as he watched her reaction to his words, but it was as though she were looking on from a distance. Surely the port had befuddled her mind. She should be feeling shock and outrage at the idea of such an improper wager, but she felt neither. She was not even surprised. Here at last was the rake, Hell-born Harry, of whose exploits Charlie had told her.

Lord Stanton said no more but continued to sip his port in a relaxed manner. Still feeling somewhat removed from reality, Anne found herself considering the wager seriously. There had been very little money for Melissa from her parents' estate, and Anne had only a competence herself. Two thousand pounds was a fortune and would guarantee a future for Melissa. It was a pity the terms of the wager would not allow the amount of the dowry to be mentioned beforehand.

Still, it would mean that what little money she did have she would be able to spend on their wardrobes, or perhaps to rent a house in a better area of London. There was one potential problem that occurred to her, and she voiced it to Lord Stanton.

"I would be a fool indeed to enter upon such a wager when a single word from you would be sufficient to destroy both our reputations and any hopes we have of establishing ourselves in Society."

Lord Stanton's half smile vanished. "If you were a man I would call you out for the imputation that I would interfere in the terms of a wager. However," he continued, his smile reappearing, "under the circumstances I will forgive you. I am afraid you must rely upon my word that I will not."

Anne was silent again. What most tempted her was that the terms of the wager were such that Melissa would gain whether she won or lost. Only for herself was there a risk. If she were to lose... Only married women could indulge in affairs with impunity. It would mean that no man would ever marry her. Not that that were likely anyway, at her age with her lack of fortune, she supposed.

Anne looked Lord Stanton over frankly, wondering why such a renowned rake was interested in having a liaison with her. He must be very bored from being in the country for a long time. Perhaps he would not even collect. Six months was a long time. By then he would be back in London and probably enamoured of another woman far more beautiful than she. Yes, that was most likely what would happen. Anne's face cleared and she opened her mouth to accept the wager, when Lord Stanton spoke with uncanny perception.

"Make no mistake, my dear. I mean to collect in full if I win. Don't deceive yourself."

His eyes travelled slowly over her with unmistakable meaning, and Anne felt an unaccountable flutter in her chest.

"But why?" she burst out. "I am not young, beautiful or wealthy."

"Because, Anne," Lord Stanton replied, using her given name, "I find you a very desirable woman. Having no intention of entering the married state, I can think of no other way to obtain what I want. If I were to simply offer you *carte blanche* you would not accept. By offering a wager, particularly one by which your cousin will gain, I have a chance. You revealed a great deal of yourself in our conversation this afternoon. I know you would honour a wager once you entered upon it. As you see, I am quite unscrupulous."

Lord Stanton smiled at Anne again, and she was aware of a feeling of intimacy between them somehow established by his use of her baptismal name and his meaningful smile. She thought again how well he fit into the opulent late-seventeenth-century furnishings of his home. So much richness and ornamentation made a very sensuous ambience. She was acutely aware of his physical presence. His arm was casually flung across the top of the sofa, revealing his shirt, and she noticed how the tightly fitting kerseymere breeches outlined the muscles of his thighs. The firelight brought out the silver glints in his hair, and his eyes seemed to caress her. Anne shook her head slightly to clear it. The situation was unthinkable! She must be foxed, she decided, setting down her glass of port. A well-brought-up woman, even one raised in a military atmosphere, would not entertain the idea of agreeing to such a wager even for a moment. And what of her promise to Sanders not to wager? As these thoughts chased each other through her mind, Lord Stanton caught her eye and saluted her with his glass provocatively, seeming to dare her to accept the wager.

"Done," she said simply, accepting his unspoken challenge.

Lord Stanton set down his glass and rose from the sofa.

"We must seal the wager," he said, taking hold of her hands and drawing her up and into his embrace. Either the unexpectedness of his actions or the port made her reactions slow, and she did not resist. His hands were warm and dry in hers a moment before he released them to clasp her closely in his arms. She felt his body moulded against hers, and then warm lips covered hers. She felt a quick sinking sensation in her stomach, and her knees weakened. Almost unaware that she was doing so, she began to return his kisses. At her response, Lord Stanton's lips became more demanding, and then suddenly he held her from him.

Anne swayed a little on her feet, but Lord Stanton held her steady. Appalled at her behaviour, Anne stared at the floor, concentrating on the intricately intertwined flowers patterning the carpet. After a moment of silence, she felt a light touch on her cheek, and Lord Stanton turned her face gently up to his.

"Good night, Anne," he said softly. "Pleasant dreams."

Anne did not reply, but pulled herself away and hurried from the room to the safety of her bedchamber.

LORD HENRY STANTON remained in the drawing room long after Anne had left, staring into the dying fire and reviewing the night's events. He was becoming more dissolute with age, not less, he feared. Whatever his companions had done, always before he had limited his attentions to married women or women of the demimonde. This was the first time he had made plans to seduce an unmarried woman of good, if not distinguished, family. He realised with some self-disgust that he would not have made the wager if Anne had male relatives to protect her.

He had not misjudged her spirit, though! Lord Henry smiled as he recalled her reaction to his proposition. Most gently bred women would have had recourse to their vinaigrettes or hartshorn, but not Anne. She was a refreshing change from the vapourish misses, bored wives and blatantly sensual Cyprians with whom he was familiar. His misgivings at the wager disappeared as he contemplated Anne's attractive qualities, and he wished he did not have to wait six months to collect. Still, it would make for an amusing season to watch Anne try to establish her ward in the upper echelons of Society. He smiled in anticipation as he rose to retire for the night, his conscience subdued.

ANNE AWOKE EARLY the next morning with the feeling that there was something unpleasant she was going to remember in a moment. Of course, the wager! She groaned and turned her face into the pillow, wishing she could remain behind the silken bed curtains forever and not have to deal with the consequences of her foolish behaviour. Whatever had possessed her!

However, much as she would have liked to stay in bed all day, she could not. She pushed back the bedcurtains and padded softly to the window. It was a white day. Heavy snow weighted down the branches of the trees, their winter garb clothing them more heavily than summer's leaves. A cloud-gray sky promised more snow. There would be no hope of escaping Longworth today. She sat on the gracefully curved window seat and continued to stare outside, the heaviness of the day matching the heaviness of her spirits.

There was no way out, not now. Charlie had taught her that one never retreated from one's gambling obligations. It simply wasn't done.

Anne rested her head in her hands and thought glumly that perhaps Lord Stanton was right, and she was not a fit chaperone for her cousin. Whatever would she do? Her only way out would be if she won. Her eyes cleared, and she straightened up. Of course! If she won, no one need ever know of the shameful wager. She would explain away the two thousand pounds to Melissa somehow and all would be well. Her spirits brightened, and she rose from the window seat, ready to face the day.

Mary entered the room with fresh water and Anne bade her good-morning cheerfully. She refused Mary's help in dressing and, after a quick wash, clad herself in a blue morning gown of valencia and a linen cap. A look at the red chinoiserie clock told her that Melissa would be awake, and she went in search of her cousin before going down to break her fast.

Anne and Melissa found that Lord Stanton had not yet come down, but the appetizing aroma coming from dishes on the side table told them that the food was ready, so they helped themselves. When Anne was halfway through a dish of kidneys, Lord Stanton made his appearance, flawlessly attired in a light green superfine coat and buff kerseymere pantaloons.

"Good morning, Miss Amberly, Miss Southwell. I trust you have both recovered from your journey?" he queried, helping himself to a large plate of food and joining them at the table.

"Yes, thank you, Lord Stanton. We were most comfortable," Anne replied.

"Oh, yes," echoed Melissa. "It would be strange if we were not comfortable. Your house is most beautiful, my lord."

Melissa had gotten over her disappointment at Lord Stanton's ordinary behaviour, and appeared to regard him in the light of an older brother.

"Perhaps you will allow me to entertain you with a tour of Longworth. I do not think the weather will allow you to depart before tomorrow."

"We should like that exceedingly," Melissa assured him.

As Anne listened to Lord Stanton talk to Melissa, she found it hard to believe that he was the same man who had drawn her into his arms and kissed her the night before. Memory of that kiss made her flush, and she glanced up quickly to see if it had been observed, but his attention was still on Melissa. Anne wondered why his kiss had disturbed her so much more than the few others she had received. She had been popular with Charlie's young fellow officers, and several had pressed their suits upon her, although none had won her heart. In Medford there had been no eligible men, and she had been content to live alone, joining in local society as one of the village spinsters.

"Anne," Melissa's voice interrupted her musings, "you have been woolgathering. Lord Stanton was just suggesting that if we are able to leave tomorrow, he would be pleased to offer us the use of one of his carriages."

"Thank you, Lord Stanton, but that will not be necessary. The carriage the squire lent us is quite satisfactory."

"I think it would be better if you accepted my offer, Miss Southwell. I know I may depend upon the discretion of my servants, but the squire's may not be as trustworthy. Were it to get about in London that you stayed here, even though it was necessitated by the weather, your reputations would be ruined. Indeed, I should warn you that if I should chance to encounter you in London I shall not recognize you, nor should you recognize me. It would be your undoing."

"I think it is most unfair," declared Melissa, her blue eyes darkening. "You have been so kind to us. I am sure you come by your reputation unjustly," she added ingenuously.

"Thank you for your defense, Miss Amberly, but I must stress the importance of not appearing to recognize me or telling anyone of your sojourn here."

"If you really think it necessary," Melissa capitulated, "but I think it a pity we cannot associate with our first friend."

"It is not quite that bad, Miss Amberly. We may be formally presented during the Season, in which case we may speak to each other, although you must not show any partiality for my company, nor I for yours."

"Perhaps after you are married you will be able to receive Lord Stanton," said Anne, looking challengingly at Lord Stanton. "If you were a married woman, there would be less danger to your reputation."

"I shall be able to, shan't I?" agreed Melissa. "I promise, I shall invite you to the first entertainment I hold."

"Thank you, Miss Amberly. I shall be honoured to attend. Perhaps Miss Southwell will allow me to escort her," Lord Stanton replied, looking questioningly at Anne.

Anne chose not to respond, commenting instead upon the sun, which had broken through a crack in the clouds. Lord Stanton accepted her change of subject with only a quirk of his eyebrows, and the remainder of the meal passed with no further awkward moments.

THE PROMISED TOUR of Longworth took most of the afternoon. Longworth had been built in the latter half of the seventeenth century, Lord Stanton informed them, by the second Marquess of Talford.

"I am fortunate," he continued, "that the three intervening holders of the title were all astute politicians who loved Longworth. They managed to stay in favour with the ruling parties and kept Longworth up well."

"Who will keep it up after you, Lord Stanton?" Anne asked somewhat presumptuously.

"My sister has three boys," he explained. "They all seem good children, so I have no worries about the fate of Longworth after my demise."

At Anne's look of surprise, he added, "Are you surprised that such a rake as myself has family? Not only do I have a sister, but I believe that she is quite fond of me. Although," he added fairly, "I know she wishes I would change my ways."

Their tour would have to be confined to the East Wing, Lord Stanton explained, as he led them up the stairs to the Long Gallery. After his holiday guests left he had had the other wings closed, and they would be bitterly cold, he said. Anne and Melissa did not miss the closed wings but were quite overwhelmed with what they did see. Anne had never been in such a great country house, and Melissa confided that the ones she had seen could not compare to the grandeur of Longworth.

The white walls were all elaborately ornamented with the sculpted and gilt decorations Anne had noticed in the Red Drawing room. Colour was provided in the carpets and the bright upholstery of the lavishly carved and heavily gilded furniture. Lord Stanton had an immense collection of paintings that lined the walls of almost every room. He brought another Fragonard to Anne's attention, but it was not in the style of the one she had seen in the red drawing room.

She looked at the portrait of a young girl closely, marvelling that the same artist could produce paintings of such different types.

"I do have two other Fragonards in the style of the first one you saw, Miss Southwell," Lord Stanton said wickedly, as he and Melissa joined Anne before the portrait. "However, they are in the wings that are presently closed. Since you are such an admirer of his works, you must come again in the summer when the other wings will be open."

Anne was going to ignore his remarks, but realised she could not in the presence of Melissa without seeming to be rude.

"Thank you, Lord Stanton," she accepted. "Perhaps I can stop on my way back to Medford this summer."

"I had hoped you would make a longer stay," he replied, his meaning evident to Anne, who could not prevent another blush.

Melissa looked at them oddly, and Anne quickly turned the conversation by asking Lord Stanton about an unusual ebony clock upon the mantelpiece. Her ploy was successful, and the rest of the tour unexceptionable.

That evening, as Lord Stanton again entertained them with amusing stories of London and the haut ton, Anne began to wonder if Lord Stanton had really been serious about the wager. There were times that day when he had seemed to tease her about it, but he had given no indication that he had meant it seriously. Perhaps he had just been amusing himself at her expense, much as Charlie and his friends had done. Men did appear to have a different sense of humour than women did, she reflected. When Lord Stanton made no attempt that evening to prevent Anne from retiring early with Melissa, she became convinced that the wager had been some kind of joke. Although, just to be on the safe side, she would be sure she won.

THE NEXT MORNING dawned clear and cold, and Lord Stanton assured them they would be able to get through the roads with no difficulty.

"I have taken the liberty of having your coachman and groom return to Medford this morning with the squire's carriage," he added. "One of my unmarked carriages is being prepared to take you to London."

"Thank you, Lord Stanton," Anne said genuinely, accepting that the precaution was for the best.

They made a good breakfast of kidneys, steak and eggs and then went to dress for their journey.

When it was time for them to depart, Anne felt oddly reluctant. She had enjoyed the short stay at Longworth, particularly the masculine company. It had been restful, too, despite Lord Stanton's teasing. Once in London, she would be overwhelmed with responsibilities.

Lord Stanton bade them good-bye in the hall as they waited for hot bricks to be placed in the carriage. Anne and Melissa thanked him once more for the shelter he had given them, while Sanders looked on in silence. Then, as Sanders adjusted the hood of Melissa's cloak about her curls, Lord Stanton leaned forward and spoke only for Anne's ears.

"Until July, my dear Anne."

CHAPTER FOUR

"MELISSA, CAN'T YOU THINK of any relatives at all, no matter how distant, who live here in London?"

"I'm sorry, Anne, there just isn't anyone. Papa was an only child, and your mother was Mama's only sister."

Anne sighed and, getting up from the Chippendale-style desk by the window, began to pace up and down the room while Melissa watched her anxiously from the sofa.

They had been in London a month now, and Anne was beginning to fear that Lord Stanton was right. They would never succeed. At first things had been deceptively easy. They had arrived in London without mishap—Lord Stanton's coachman had taken them to a respectable hotel. From there Anne had contacted an agent, and they were able to rent a town house with a good address for a reasonable rate since the Season had not yet begun. It was small, with only one drawing room, but it was attractively furnished, and both she and Melissa were pleased with it. They had staffed the house well at minimal expense by hiring servants who had little experience. Their butler was a former footman in his early twenties, their footman a young lad from the country and one of their housemaids, a former scullery maid. What they lacked in experience they made up for in willingness, and on the whole, Anne was satisfied with their staff. Only in the matter of their cook was Anne not content. After their first meal of underdone lamb, she found herself thinking wistfully of the excellently prepared meals at Longworth.

Transportation had been their next concern. Their butler, Benton, had told them they would need a carriage, and had undertaken to find one for them. He had discovered a used town carriage in good shape, and although she shuddered at the cost, Anne had purchased it. This had, of course, necessitated the acquisition of horses to draw the carriage. Benton again came to their rescue, locating a rather unmatched pair at a very reasonable price. Although Melissa was dubious, Anne had cared more about their sturdiness than the way they looked, and was grateful for the money she saved.

The matter of their residence taken care of, Anne and Melissa had turned their attention to their wardrobes. After a conference with Sanders, they decided that Sanders would make their morning gowns and night dresses but that they would have their walking dresses and ball gowns made by a modiste. Melissa already had a fairly fashionable wardrobe, which needed only a few additions, but Anne had to purchase an entire new wardrobe. She knew that if she presented a shabby appearance it would not reflect well on Melissa. Although the rates charged by London modistes shocked her, Anne spent several delightful mornings with Melissa, selecting materials and styles from the wealth of choices available in the London shops.

Then their luck had ceased. With no one to sponsor them, she and Melissa had no way of being invited to even the smallest rout or card party. They had remained in their well-staffed town house, in their new clothes, alone. Anne had racked her brains to remember someone she knew who might be in London, but without success. Melissa was her only hope. She resumed her questioning.

"Then how about friends? There must be *someone* in London with whom you had acquaintance."

Melissa concentrated, her normally smooth forehead wrinkled in thought.

"No, we spent all year at Amberly Hall. Papa didn't care for Town. We were neighbours of Lord Franklin, but he and Lady Franklin will not arrive until later, if they come to London for the Season at all this year. It will be another year before his eldest daughter makes her come-out."

Melissa looked at Anne apologetically, unable to come up with any other ideas.

Anne put her hand to her head in exasperation, displacing her attractive muslin cap and giving herself a slightly saucy look.

"There must be some avenue we are overlooking. Papa would..." Her voice trailed off. "That's it! There must be some military families in residence. If only I had kept in better contact."

"Perhaps one of the servants would know," ventured Melissa.

"Of course," Anne cried, pulling the bell rope. "Ask Benton to come in," she said to the young footman who answered her ring.

"I remember when I interviewed Benton that he said he had formerly served a military gentleman," Anne said to Melissa. "Surely he will know who is in residence in London."

Benton, a slender young man with sandy hair and freckles, was most anxious to help his young mistresses. He knew that few other people would have given him an opportunity to advance to the position of butler, and he wished to prove his gratitude.

"If you will name some of the officers with whom you were acquainted, ma'am, perhaps I could tell you if they are in residence," he suggested.

Anne named several without success, but was lucky with her sixth try, Captain Halcott.

"There is a Colonel Halcott, ma'am. Might that be the same family?"

"Yes, no doubt it is," Anne replied delightedly. "It would be odd if he had not advanced in rank since I knew him. I will send a note round to Mrs. Halcott immediately."

Returning to her desk, she quickly wrote a note, which Benton dispatched the footman with.

While they waited for a response, Melissa went to inspect some parcels that had arrived from the milliners, hoping that one of them contained her new gypsy hat and veil. Anne, realising that Mrs. Halcott was probably their last hope to find someone willing to assist them in gaining entrance into Society, was unable to interest herself in the parcels. She remained in the drawing room, alternately pacing the floor and sitting on an uncomfortable ladder-backed chair, twisting her skirt between her hands. Why hadn't she thought of this before she left Medford? And why hadn't she kept in contact with her former friends?

Fortunately for her state of mind, a response to her note came within the hour in the form of a call by Mrs. Halcott herself. As Benton proudly announced her, she went immediately to Anne and embraced her fondly.

"My dear Anne. I was so surprised to receive your note. Seven years! What are you doing and how is it you've never married?" she asked, holding Anne at arm's length and inspecting her critically. "You are certainly in good looks," she added, taking in Anne's appearance in her new leaf-green frock trimmed with lace and tied beneath her breasts with a white rib-band.

Anne smiled warmly at Mrs. Halcott and returned her compliments. Mrs. Halcott did not appear to have aged at all in the past years. Her brown hair was still unstreaked by grey, and her plump figure looked most fashionable in a puce muslin morning gown. They sat down together on the sofa, while Anne explained her long silence to Mrs. Halcott.

"I'm afraid I've lived a very retired life since Papa's and Charlie's deaths," she said. "I just couldn't interest myself in Society."

"Of course, I understand." Mrs. Halcott sympathized. "But you are still a young woman, Anne. I am glad to see you have decided to come back into Society."

"It's not on my account," Anne confessed, proceeding to outline her predicament to Mrs. Halcott.

Mrs. Halcott frowned thoughtfully. "Amberly—he resigned his commission after inheriting a baronetcy, did he not? Well, her father had a title, if she does not. That should help. And if Melissa is as beautiful as you say, there should be no difficulty introducing her into Society. I would be more than glad to help. But you know, my dear, we do not move in the exclusive circles of the ton, only on the outer fringes. Vouchers to Almack's will be out of the question, I am afraid."

"Indeed, I did not expect to enter the inner circle," Anne assured her. "I would be most grateful for us to be included in any Society at all."

"Well, then, introduce me to your cousin and let us make some plans," Mrs. Halcott said practically. "Since your ward is not yet out, and the Season does not begin for another month, we must limit your engagements to small routs and supper parties at first. I will, of course, hold a coming-out ball for your ward once the Season begins."

"It is too generous of you," Anne protested, feeling a twinge of guilt at Mrs. Halcott's readiness to assume the responsibility of introducing them to the ton after her years of failing to keep in touch.

"Nonsense. I never had any daughters myself, only my scapegrace son. I will enjoy it. Besides, Colonel Halcott would never forgive me if I did not do my best for Major Southwell's daughter," she said, patting Anne's hand. "Now, call in Melissa."

Mrs. Halcott took to Melissa immediately. "The only thing wrong with you is that you are *too* beautiful," she said, taking in the delicate figure, glossy hair and finely chiseled features. "You are going to stir jealousy in some breasts. I'm not sure I would be willing to sponsor you myself if I had a marriageable daughter," she admitted candidly.

Melissa blushed and looked at the floor, embarrassed by such a frank assessment of her beauty.

"I am holding a small supper party this Thursday evening," Mrs. Halcott continued. "Just a few officers and their wives, but it will serve as an introduction for you. Now, I must be going. Until Thursday."

They rose and, embracing Anne fondly once more, Mrs. Halcott hastened away, leaving her new protégées feeling quite overwhelmed by their sudden good fortune.

ANNE AND MELISSA dressed with great care the evening of Mrs. Halcott's supper party, wishing to do her credit. Melissa looked enchantingly innocent in a white muslin frock with bodice *à l'enfant*. The hem and short puffed sleeves were embellished with flowers embroidered in a blue that matched her eyes, and she had threaded a blue ribband through her black curls. Anne had chosen a striped yellow, red and green lutestring dress with a short train and square décolletage. As befitted her status as Melissa's chaperone, she wore a cornette over her coiled hair.

"You'll do," approved Sanders, as she assisted them into their pelisses. "No wagers, mind you," she admonished Anne, not quite trusting her to keep her promise when in the company of military gentlemen.

"No wagers," Anne assured her.

Melissa spoke thoughtfully as she drew on her gloves, an idea just occurring to her.

"You don't ever wager anymore, Anne. I haven't even heard you wager with yourself. Have you been feeling quite the thing?" she asked, looking distressed that she might not have noticed Anne was suffering from an indisposition.

"I am fine. I am just endeavoring to remember Sanders's strictures on my behaviour," Anne replied lightly. "I *am* your chaperone, and must behave accordingly."

She hoped none of the inner turmoil caused by Melissa's remarks showed upon her face. The reckless wager she had entered upon with Lord Stanton had cured her of her habit as Sanders's admonitions never could. He might only have been having fun with her—she suspected it was so, since she had heard nothing from him—but it did not excuse her entering into such an improper wager. Her behaviour had been inexcusably lax. She was relieved when the footman informed them their carriage was ready, allowing the subject to be dropped.

The Halcotts' town house was only a short distance away, so they arrived within a few minutes, to be warmly welcomed by the Halcotts. Colonel Halcott, a heavy man of florid complexion and bluff manners, embraced both girls heartily, assuring Anne that there was nothing he and Mrs. Halcott would not do for the daughter of Major Southwell. Anne thanked him prettily, pleased by his remembrances of her father. Mrs. Halcott led them into the drawing room to wait until the rest of the guests had arrived.

"What a beautiful room!" Melissa exclaimed, bringing a pleased smile to Mrs. Halcott's face.

Anne agreed as she looked around the tastefully decorated room. White plasterwork in the form of graceful arches adorned the doorways and the edges of the ceilings, contrasting with the blue of the walls. The arches were also displayed on the backs of the chairs and other furniture, giving an overall effect of delicacy and lightness.

Mrs. Halcott introduced Anne and Melissa to the other guests as they arrived. Her small party consisted of eighteen persons, most of them older, but her son, Lieutenant Halcott, and his friend, Captain Leslie, provided companionship for Anne and Melissa. At supper, Anne found herself seated between the captain and an older officer of the Hussars. Melissa and Lieutenant Halcott were seated across from her.

Lieutenant Halcott, a well-favoured young man with brown hair and eyes, was instantly and obviously smitten with Melissa. Anne was vastly entertained by his attentions to her at the supper table. He continually plied Melissa with those dishes he thought she would prefer, not hesitating to call down the table for a particular delicacy he wished to offer her.

"I see your cousin has made a conquest already," said Captain Leslie from her side, and Anne was recalled to her manners. She smiled at the handsome blonde captain in the uniform of a Rifles officer beside her.

"Yes, I only hope that Mrs. Halcott will forgive us if some of her guests go hungry," she said, looking at the array of dishes before Melissa.

"Never fear, you may be sure the other guests will help themselves quickly when the second remove is placed on the table," he said, his blue eyes twinkling.

"I understand you are Major Southwell's daughter," he continued. "It may be of interest to you to know that I served under him in Egypt. If I am not bringing back unhappy memories," he added contritely.

"Oh, no, Captain Leslie," Anne assured him. "It is quite all right. Indeed, I would like to talk to someone who served with him there."

"Then I hope you will allow me to call upon you one morning that I may do so."

"Of course. I shall look forward to it," returned Anne, pleased to be making a new friend.

The Hussars officer on her other side addressed a remark to her, and she turned to him. The rest of the supper passed very pleasantly. After the coffee was served, Mrs. Halcott rose, indicating it was time for the women to retire and leave the gentlemen to their port.

The women conversed amicably in the blue drawing room as they waited for the gentlemen to rejoin them. Anne chose a seat in a corner of the room, intending to watch Melissa and see how she conducted herself, but she was foiled in her plans by Mrs. Singleton. Mrs. Singleton, a garrulous elderly widow, seated herself next to Anne and proceeded to describe in great detail the many illnesses she suffered from.

Anne was relieved when the gentlemen rejoined them, hoping for rescue from Mrs. Singleton. She had not long to wait, for Captain Leslie caught the desperate plea in her eyes and gallantly came to her aid. He neatly steered the conversation into other waters, which freed Anne to observe the other guests.

Lieutenant Halcott once again attached himself to Melissa, oblivious to his social duties. Mrs. Halcott, not wishing her son's lack of attention to the other guests to draw more attention than it already had, requested Anne and Melissa to entertain the company with music. Happy to completely escape Mrs. Singleton, Anne seated herself at the Broadwood pianoforte, and Captain Leslie volunteered his services turning pages. Melissa stood behind Anne and sang a light air in her soft soprano. She was soon joined by Lieutenant Halcott, who added his tenor. Mrs. Halcott surveyed the couples complacently, satisfied that she had begun her duties as sponsor very well.

THAT NIGHT, as Melissa prepared for bed, she and Anne discussed the evening.

"I am glad we came to London after all," Melissa confided as Sanders unfastened her frock and helped her into her nightrail. "I did have some misgivings this past month, but this night was quite enjoyable. Lieutenant Halcott was most kind, and Captain Leslie was very attentive to you. Wouldn't it be wonderful if we both made matches before the Season is over?"

"I have no doubt that you will," Anne replied from her perch on the bed, "but as for me, I am quite an ape-leader at nine-and-twenty."

"We'll see. Not all gentlemen prefer young misses," Sanders said, well aware of Anne's quiet, more mature beauty.

"Sandy is right," Melissa confirmed, seating herself on a stool as Sanders began to brush her hair. "I am sure you will receive an offer before the end of the Season."

"Don't worry about me," Anne replied, rising to retire to her own bedchamber. "I am quite content to remain as I am."

But even as she said the words, a face floated before her mind's eye, and it was the dark one of Lord Stanton, not the fair one of Captain Leslie.

MRS. HALCOTT ESCORTED ANNE and Melissa to several small gatherings during the next few weeks, as they prepared for their full plunge into Society when the Season opened in April. Lieutenant Halcott and Captain Leslie were most accommodating, serving as willing escorts to affairs they normally found tedious. They went to the circulating library, the Tower, and for walks in Hyde Park during the unfashionable hours. Anne found the company of the officers agreeable and undemanding, feeling younger and more carefree than she had in years. She had feared that Melissa might make too much of Lieutenant Halcott's devotion to her, but she seemed to regard him in a sisterly fashion, which quite put Anne's mind at ease.

Melissa's come-out ball was planned for the first week of the Season. That way, Mrs. Halcott had explained, there would not be many competing balls given by higher-ranking hostesses, and they might have a few more titled guests attend. Melissa did not seem worried about her coming debut, but Anne was. The ball would be their real introduction into Society—a foretaste of the rest of the Season. If, for some reason, Melissa was not well received, it would be difficult for her to make a good match. Anne solicited Mrs. Halcott's aid in choosing their gowns and accessories for the ball, and found her money slipping away faster than she had planned.

A week before the ball, Anne made a call on her banker to procure more funds. It was taking more to maintain an establishment in London than she had calculated. She sighed as she waited for Mr. Collings to reappear in the small office and looked through the open door to where Sanders waited in the outer office. Presently, Mr. Collings returned, placing the money Anne had requested on the desk.

"Thank you for waiting, Miss Southwell," he said in his precise voice. "Here are the funds you require."

He sat behind his desk. "What did you wish me to do with the two thousand pounds we received from Miss Amberly's uncle?"

Anne could not repress a momentary start of surprise. Since Melissa had no living uncle, it could only be the two thousand pounds from Lord Stanton. She collected herself immediately.

"Yes, thank you for informing me, Mr. Collings," she said softly, aware of Sanders's presence in the outer office. "The money is to constitute my ward's dowry. Please place it in a separate account for that purpose."

"Very well, Miss Southwell," Mr. Collings replied, as Anne rose to leave. He rose also and bowed. "Good day."

"Good day," Anne responded, and left the banker's office to rejoin Sanders, her face reflecting the shock she felt. During the past month in London she had come near to forgetting the wager with Lord Stanton. Indeed, she had become convinced that he had never been serious, but had only been amusing himself at her expense. The two thousand pounds deposited to the account made her uncomfortably aware that Lord Stanton *was* serious and had every intention of holding her to the wager.

Disturbed by these thoughts, she nearly ran into a passer-by on the street as she left the bank and tripped stepping into the carriage. Sanders, noticing Anne's distracted air, hoped that she was not having financial troubles.

AT HIS PALLADIAN-STYLE town house in St. James's Square, Lord Stanton was sustaining a morning call from his sister, Lady Brookfield. Lady Brookfield, an attractive brunette clad in a lace-trimmed yellow jaconet frock, was quizzing her brother on his early arrival in London.

"What brings you to Town so early, Harry? It's not like you to appear before the Season is half over, particularly when the Prince is still in Brighton. Have you fallen out with him?"

"No," Lord Stanton denied, leaning back in his comfortable wing chair, crossing his booted feet. "I haven't seen Prinny since last December. I just came up from Longworth. Thought I might see the Season through this year."

"Don't tell me you are considering settling down," Lady Brookfield said, looking at her handsome brother sceptically. She was fully aware of his feelings about the Season. He had told her often enough how he disliked having each year's new crop of misses thrown at him. The highest sticklers did not receive her brother, but the majority were not so choosy. Money was a great cleanser.

"No," he replied, dousing any faint hopes she might have entertained. "I've no need to do that when you have me well supplied with heirs. Although I will confess that my reasons for being in Town do involve a woman."

Lady Brookfield shook her head in annoyance and clicked her tongue in a most unladylike manner.

"I should have known. Who is it this time? An actress, Cyprian or one of my married friends? Not that last, I hope. It was most uncomfortable when you were involved with Lady Cranburne."

"Really, dear sister," Lord Stanton said with a mocking smile, "a respectable woman like yourself should not know of such things, much less speak of them."

"How can I help knowing, with 'Hell-born Harry' for a brother?" she said with spirit.

"For that cut, dear Caro, I am not going to tell you who it is, but leave you guessing," he teased.

"Beast!" she rejoined, rising to take her leave. "You are far too confident in your dealings with women. Someday I hope the tables are turned and you will have your comeuppance."

"Very well, I shall repent," Lord Stanton said, rising also and walking to the door with her. "And to show my good will I offer my services as your escort this Season to those affairs Brookfield does not care for."

"I shall hold you to it," accepted Lady Brookfield, looking at her brother sharply as she bade him good-bye. It was most unlike Harry to have any interest in the entertainments of the more staid haut ton. He preferred those of the Carlton House set. He must be up to something. She would have to keep her eyes open.

Lord Stanton knew his sister was highly suspicious of his motives, but chose not to enlighten her. Anne must have a fair chance, and he could not risk even his sister being aware of his interest in Anne, at least not yet.

He stood idly by the marble fireplace for a moment after his sister's departure, wondering how Anne was faring in her attempts to establish her cousin in Society so far. He would have liked to have seen the expression on her face when she found out about the two thousand pounds he had deposited to her account. It was going to be a most entertaining Season, even if he couldn't share his amusement with anyone. Yes, most entertaining, win or lose.

CHAPTER FIVE

THE REMAINDER OF THE WEEK passed quickly. Preparing for Melissa's ball left Anne little time to worry about the two thousand pounds. The night of the ball they arrived at the Halcotts' town house early, so that Mrs. Halcott could inspect their toilettes. It was of the utmost importance that everything be correct. Melissa was appropriately dressed in a high-waisted white muslin gown with short puff sleeves and a rounded décolletage. The pointed toes of her satin slippers peeped from beneath the hem, and she carried a matching white satin reticule containing her fan, vinaigrette and scent bottle. A sapphire necklace at her throat provided a touch of colour, along with a matching sapphire fillet, which shone in her glossy black curls.

Anne wore a green silk dress which opened in front to expose a decorative petticoat of blonde lace. Long sleeves of spider-net fell loosely over her arms to spread gracefully over her hands from narrow waist bands. She had abandoned her usual classical coils to bunch her hair in curls from an opening in her lace cap. Anne had little jewellery, and wore only a modest necklace of amber.

"Two diamonds of the first water, as my son would say," pronounced Mrs. Halcott in satisfaction. She was in excellent looks herself in a red velvet robe with gold fringe around the hem and a matching red-and-gold turban. "Don't be nervous," she chided. "I predict you will be unqualified successes."

She took them to inspect the ballroom, which had been formed by opening two rooms together. Most of the furniture had been removed, and a profusion of potted plants and artistically arranged flowers had been placed about.

"I considered having a theme," she explained, "but decided that I would prefer the guests' attention to be on the two of you and not the decorations."

Anne and Melissa barely had time to admire Mrs. Halcott's efforts when it was time for them to go stand with the Halcotts to greet the guests. Anne turned to reassure Melissa but saw that she was less nervous than she was herself. As they were presented to the guests, Anne was surprised by the number who came, and their social ranks. Mrs. Halcott had outdone herself. There were, of course, many military gentlemen present, but there were also a marquess, an earl, a viscount and two barons. Anne saw with satisfaction that Melissa received many admiring looks from the men. The women were less admiring and gave both Anne and Melissa some sharp, searching glances. One young lady in particular, a tall, strikingly beautiful brunette in rose silk, was barely civil.

"Don't mind Lady Conliffe," whispered Mrs. Halcott to Anne. "She only fears that her reputation as the Dark Beauty is in jeopardy with the appearance of Melissa on the scene. She has held the title the past two Seasons."

Anne was relieved when they were able to leave their places by the door and join the guests. She hoped she would remember all the names of the people to whom she had been presented. It would be easier for Melissa, who was more accustomed to social functions. Melissa was led out to begin the first dance, and Anne went to sit with the chaperones at the edge of the dance floor. She was trying to match the faces of the guests with the names when Mrs. Halcott joined her, in the company of Captain Leslie.

"I am your chaperone tonight, dear," she said. "You must enjoy yourself and dance. May I present Captain Leslie as a suitable partner?"

Anne smiled at the captain, accepting his offer to stand up with her. After the first set with the captain, who also wrote his name down for the supper dance, Anne found to her surprise that she did not lack for partners. Her second partner was none other than the Earl of Millbank, an exquisitely dressed young gentleman in a high-collared blue coat, yellow waistcoat and a red cravat swathed so tightly about his neck that he was unable to move his head. Anne found it difficult not to stare at such magnificence, but the young earl evidently took her looks to be admiring ones and wrote his name down for another dance.

It was Melissa, however, who was the undoubted success of the evening. Every single gentleman present, including many of the married ones, vied for a space on her card. Melissa seemed unaffected by her popularity, showing preference for no particular gentleman, and allowing no one more than one dance. Her modest behaviour quickly earned her the approbation of the chaperones, who pronounced her a prettily behaved chit.

Anne noticed her popularity with both pride and relief. Her decision to bring Melissa to London for a Season had been the correct one. A member of the nobility was even showing interest in her ward. Anne had remarked the way Viscount Woolbridge had been struck by her beauty, his eyes following her wherever she went.

Happily, Anne danced every dance. She was unused to such exertion, however, and was relieved when Captain Leslie claimed her for the supper dance. He seated her at an empty table in the supper room and went to procure them plates of food.

"Your cousin will undoubtedly be labeled one of the Season's Incomparables after tonight," the captain predicted to Anne as he placed their food on the table and sat down. "You will have to be very cautious."

"Why is that, Captain Leslie?" inquired Anne, applying herself to a venison pastry the captain had selected for her.

"Such beauty inspires both the best and the worst qualities of people to come to the fore. You will have to guard against the dishonourable intentions of some of the men and the jealous spite of some of the women."

Captain Leslie nodded in the direction of the table where Lady Conliffe sat with Viscount Woolbridge. "Particularly hers. Your cousin has quite cast her into the shade tonight, and she will not easily forgive that."

"Thank you for the warning," Anne replied, "but I do not see how someone of Melissa's gentle personality could inspire too much hate."

"I think you do not know much of Society," Captain Leslie said, smiling. "I also think it is one of your charms," he added, lest he sound critical.

Anne accepted his compliment and changed the subject, but in her heart she suspected Captain Leslie was correct. His words were an echo of Lord Stanton's. Perhaps she had been over-confident. Society was a dangerous place, particularly for one whose standing was as precarious as hers or Melissa's. No doubt Lord Stanton had been thinking of such problems when he made the wager with her. It wasn't only their lack of high social standing that would make her task difficult. She wondered if Lord Stanton were in Town for the Season. He must be if he had put the money in her account. She knew better than to expect that Mrs. Halcott would invite someone of Lord Stanton's reputation, but still she had watched for him.

"A penny for your thoughts," Captain Leslie interrupted, his blue eyes quizzical.

"I'm sorry, Captain Leslie," Anne apologized. "I was just thinking of what you said earlier. I had not realised, when I made plans to bring Melissa here for the Season, that it would be quite so difficult."

Captain Leslie looked penitent. "I had not meant to alarm you, Miss Southwell. Don't repine too much upon what I said. Lady Conliffe may be disgruntled by Miss Amberly's appearance in Society, but there is little she can do beyond disparaging her to her acquaintances."

"Perhaps not, Captain Leslie, but I will be careful to avoid crossing her, just the same."

Another couple joined them at their table, and the conversation turned to more general subjects.

After the break for supper, Anne returned to the ballroom, feeling rested and ready to dance again. Lord Woolbridge, the young viscount who had seemed so taken with Melissa, solicited Anne's hand for the gavotte. He exerted himself to be quite charming, and Anne suspected it was because of her connexion with Melissa. She looked at him speculatively as they went through the steps of the dance. He was a handsome young man in his early twenties, with thick chestnut hair, hazel eyes and a pleasant, open countenance. Perhaps this would be the titled gentleman for her ward. She resolved to ask her sponsor about him immediately after the dance was over.

Mrs. Halcott had a great deal of good to say about the young viscount.

"He is but recently ascended to the title, but he takes his duties quite seriously, I hear. He has a considerable fortune, so money would not be a factor to him. He has been very attentive to Lady Conliffe, but nothing was ever announced. He would be an excellent match for your cousin if he comes up to scratch."

Anne felt less sanguine about the prospect after hearing he was connected with Lady Conliffe. She didn't think that lady would relinquish her claim on the viscount easily. Well, there was time for other gentlemen to show interest in Melissa. The Season was just beginning. She ceased worrying about Melissa and commenced to enjoy the rest of the evening.

In the early hours of the morning an exhausted but satisfied Mrs. Halcott saw the last of her guests depart.

"I could not have asked for things to go better. It was an unqualified success! You should have heard the questions I was bombarded with by the mamas of Melissa's dance partners," she said to Anne. "Mark my words, you won't lack for invitations after tonight. You will not miss being at Almacks."

Anne and Melissa expressed their heartfelt thanks to Mrs. Halcott and prepared to go home, tired but happy.

"Don't forget we are to attend the opera Friday," Mrs. Halcott reminded them. "An appearance there will put the seal on your success. Many of the haut ton not present tonight will have heard of Melissa by then, and no doubt we shall receive many requests for introductions."

THE NEXT MORNING Benton was kept busy accepting flowers and cards from the gentlemen who had danced with his mistresses the night before.

"Isn't this exciting!" enthused Melissa as two more young officers departed after making a call. "I never dreamed we would be so popular."

Anne smiled at Melissa. Melissa's unselfconsciousness was one of her most attractive qualities. She seemed totally unaware of the beautiful picture she presented in her pink sprigged muslin morning gown with a matching ribband in her hair.

"No, Melissa, I am not one whit surprised by your success. Although I am surprised that an ape-leader such as myself was singled out for so much attention."

"I was not. You are not ancient, Anne. You are a very beautiful woman."

Their conversation was interrupted by Benton announcing yet two more callers.

"Captain Leslie and Lieutenant Halcott," he intoned.

After the officers presented their compliments, they begged to be allowed to take Anne and Melissa for a drive in the park that afternoon.

"You must be seen during the Promenade now that you have been presented," Lieutenant Halcott explained.

"You know it will greatly enhance our reputations to be seen with the new Incomparables," added Captain Leslie teasingly.

"As it will ours to be seen with two such handsome officers," returned Anne. "Thank you, we shall be pleased to go."

"Viscount Woolbridge," announced Benton.

Viscount Woolbridge entered, immaculate in a blue superfine coat with plated buttons, striped waistcoat, tight-fitting pantaloons and shining Hessians. He frowned slightly at seeing the uniformed officers already in possession of the drawing room, but greeted them politely before returning his attention to Melissa.

"May I hope that you will allow me the pleasure of taking you for a drive this afternoon?" he asked.

"Thank you, Lord Woolbridge," Melissa replied, "but we are already promised to drive with Captain Leslie and Lieutenant Halcott."

Lord Woolbridge was too well bred to allow his irritation to show.

"Tomorrow afternoon, then?" he persisted.

"Yes, I should be delighted," Melissa assured him.

Viscount Woolbridge seated himself across from Melissa and gazed at her as though he could not get enough of her beauty. Lieutenant Halcott looked far from pleased at having a rival for Miss Amberly's attention, particularly one with a title. Anne and Captain Leslie exchanged glances of amusement, but Melissa seemed unaware of the developing rivalry. When their fifteen minutes were up, the officers reluctantly departed, taking the viscount with them. Anne and Melissa informed Benton they were not home to any more callers and retired to rest and have something to eat before their drive.

ANNE AND MELISSA WERE READY promptly at a quarter to five, Anne in a simple green poplin frock and fur-edged curricle cloak of cashmere, Melissa in a yellow muslin frock and green sarcenet pelisse fringed in orange. Matching straw bonnets completed their outfits.

Lieutenant Halcott had brought his parents' landau so the couples could be seated together and enjoy the drive. This was Anne and Melissa's first excursion to Hyde Park during the fashionable hour of five, and they looked about interestedly. Progress was very slow, for vehicles and horsemen were constantly halting in order to greet acquaintances. One of the first acquaintances they encountered was Lord Millbank, driving a young girl in his fashionable yellow phaeton. Melissa admired the earl's matched white horses, decked out in orange and green rosettes. They stopped to exchange greetings, and Lord Millbank introduced the girl beside him, who proved to be his younger sister, Lady Amelia Millbank. Anne felt compassion for this sister, who spoke in a very soft voice and appeared to be very shy. She was dressed attractively in a pale blue sarcenet carriage dress and matching pelisse, but her mousy hair and lack of countenance made her seem to fade into the background.

Melissa was apparently quite taken with her, however, and did not hesitate to make plans for furthering their acquaintance.

"Lady Millbank, would you care to accompany me to the circulating library tomorrow morning?" she asked.

Lady Amelia flushed with pleasure. "Yes, I should like that exceedingly, Miss Amberly," she replied.

As the two girls arranged a time, Anne felt some remorse. Why had it not occurred to her that Melissa must have felt the lack of a friend her own age? Well, Melissa seemed to have supplied the lack herself. In her pleasure, Anne smiled brilliantly at Lord Millbank, who preened in the light of the smile, feeling sure it was his new canary-and cerulean-blue-striped waistcoat that caused it.

The vehicles soon had to pull away from each other, and they continued on their slow progress around the park. The next acquaintances they encountered were Viscount Woolbridge and Lady Conliffe, in a shiny blue curricle drawn by beautifully matched bays. Lady Conliffe, dressed attractively in a pink cambric dress with a waistcoat bosom, a velvet pelisse and a becoming cottage bonnet, looked smug in her place beside the viscount. As the occupants of the two vehicles exchanged greetings, Anne's eye was caught by a familiar-looking form in a black curricle not far away, and she failed to respond to a question from Captain Leslie. Captain Leslie followed her gaze.

"Ah, I see you are not immune to the appearance of Lord Stanton, better known as 'Hell-born Harry.'"

"Is he so dreadful?" inquired Anne innocently. "And who is his beautiful companion?" she asked, looking at the woman beside him, a blonde whose hair was so pale as to appear silver.

"That is Lady Parnell. Really, Miss Southwell, you should not show so much interest in the premier rake of the realm," he teased.

"Indeed not, Miss Southwell," interrupted Lady Conliffe from the phaeton beside them. "It will be thought unbecomingly fast, even in one of your years."

Anne smiled at Lady Conliffe's gibe, but did not allow herself to retaliate.

"Thank you, Lady Conliffe. I will try to keep your warning in mind," she replied, and turned her attention from the glossy black curricle, at least outwardly. Inwardly, however, she found herself consumed with curiosity about Lord Stanton's ravishing companion, as well as strangely hurt. She scolded herself. After all, Lord Stanton had made it very clear that it was for their benefit he would not acknowledge them in London. But the joy had gone out of the day for Anne, and she was relieved when they completed their turn about the Park to return home.

THE NEXT DAY, Anne remained at home while Melissa went for her drive with Viscount Woolbridge. The viscount had gravely assured Anne of his driving abilities while he was waiting for Melissa to appear, and promised to return her safely. Anne just as gravely assured him of her confidence in his skill, thinking what a handsome appearance he made in his blue coat, buff vest and buckskins. The viscount appeared no less impressed by the appearance of Melissa when she came into the room clad in a chemise-dress of dotted muslin trimmed with lace and tied under her breasts with a red ribband. A gypsy hat with a white veil sat on her curls, and a white sarcenet scarf was draped gracefully about her shoulders. The viscount gazed at her adoringly a full half minute before he was able to bid her good-afternoon.

Anne stood in the window as they departed, watching the viscount hand Melissa carefully into his curricle. She turned to Sanders, who sat quietly working on a muslin morning gown for Melissa.

"Melissa and the viscount make a handsome couple, do they not?"

"I still say you should have gone with them for propriety's sake," Sanders replied with some asperity.

"Perhaps I should have," agreed Anne, "but his interest in Melissa seems quite respectable. He treats her like a piece of delicate porcelain. And Melissa appears to return his regard."

Sanders stopped sewing and looked at Anne more kindly.

"I think Melissa is enjoying her first Season too much to make any decisions. The Season has just begun. She may meet other gentlemen yet. But you have done very well for Melissa, so far," she acknowledged.

"Not I, but Mrs. Halcott," Anne said fairly. "I know I should not be making plans yet, but I do so wish Melissa to make a good match. I cannot afford a second Season," she added, thinking, *nor will I be a proper person to chaperone her if she does not make a match this Season.*

Sanders looked at Anne with some concern. "I hope you are not jeopardizing your own income to present Melissa this Season. There is no need. A girl of Melissa's beauty and breeding will make a good match despite her lack of money."

Anne wondered uncomfortably if Sanders suspected something from the day at the bank. She wished she had not started the conversation, or that Sanders was not quite so familiar in her speech. Somehow she always made Anne very aware of her shortcomings as a chaperone.

"No, I have not endangered my income," she replied rather shortly, and left the room with the excuse of conferring with the cook about the week's menus. Sanders looked after her thoughtfully, convinced something was bothering Anne, and hoping it was not serious.

FRIDAY, ANNE AND MELISSA dressed for the opera with great care, aware that they would be on view to much of the haut ton, which they would have few opportunities to meet elsewhere. Anne chose a trained evening gown edged in trim of an Egyptian motif worn over a petticoat of white satin trimmed in gold. She wore a gold net on her hair, and at her neck was her simple amber necklace. Melissa was clad in a high-waisted gown of white sarcenet which fell about her slender form in classical folds. She carried a large white swans-down muff and wore a fillet of amethysts in her curls. Sanders looked them over critically, making several minute adjustments to their costumes before she was satisfied.

The Halcotts called for them in their large town carriage, Mrs. Halcott looking well in a purple velvet robe and modest tiara of diamonds in her elaborately dressed hair. They arrived at Covent Garden unfashionably early so that her charges would have the opportunity to look about the opera house before the performance began. As they entered the box, Anne was grateful for Mrs. Halcott's foresight, for she found herself hard put not to gawk at the magnificence like the provincial she was. Gleaming chandeliers illuminated the interior brightly, and the tiers of boxes and galleries decorated in crimson, white and gold looked quite majestic.

Soon, however, Anne's attention was diverted from the furnishings to the people. The other boxes began to fill with women wearing glittering jewels, and the pit filled with rowdy young bucks and people from the lower classes. Mrs. Halcott informed them in a low voice of the identity of some of the other patrons, pointing out the many titled gentlemen present. A familiar head of silver-blonde hair in a box across from theirs caught Anne's attention.

"Who is the beautiful woman with the pale blonde hair across from us?" she asked Mrs. Halcott, knowing quite well what the answer would be, and avoiding looking at Melissa.

"She is Lady Parnell. And that is Lord Stanton, the Marquess of Talford, who has just joined her. He is quite rich and is very well favoured, but he is also very dissolute. Oh, dear," she fretted, "he appears to have noticed Melissa and is looking this way."

Anne could not resist a glance to ascertain if he were indeed looking their way. She was not prepared for the thrill that went down her spine as she found herself looking directly into his eyes. He was standing behind Lady Parnell, and Anne could see he was impeccably clad in black silk knee breeches, white waistcoat, black coat and a *chapeau bras* beneath his arm.

"I hope he doesn't ask to be introduced to Melissa between acts," worried Mrs. Halcott. "I don't know what I should do. Many of the highest-ranking hostesses don't receive him, although he is close to the Prince."

Anne doubted that Lord Stanton would come to their box but, perversely, found herself wishing he would. Let him see, at least, that she *was* establishing Melissa in Society.

This last became very clear after the first act, as the Halcotts' box became full of Melissa's admirers. Several gentlemen asked to be presented to her, not a few of whom were of the nobility. When she dared, Anne stole looks at Lord Stanton's box, but he seemed totally absorbed in his beautiful companion, and never again did she catch his eye upon her.

Anne was unaware that her stolen glances at Lord Stanton's box had caught the attention of a dark-haired beauty sitting not far from Lord Stanton. Lady Conliffe, furious at seeing much of her usual court stopping in the Halcotts' box, was observing them very closely, and noticed Anne's frequent interest in Lord

Stanton and his partner. Lady Conliffe had a very thoughtful look on her face when the second act began, and it remained throughout the opera.

Anne, unaware of the close scrutiny she was under, enjoyed the remaining two acts of Handel's *Giulio Cesare* thoroughly. She had a genuine love of music, and appreciated the beautiful voice of Gertrude Mara, who was playing the part of Cleopatra. Melissa, in common with most of the patrons, was more interested in observing the people.

Anne and Melissa returned home that night full of their success, feeling that the major hurdles to their establishment in Society had been overcome.

CHAPTER SIX

LORD STANTON PUT AN EXPRESSION of impenetrable politeness on his face and allowed his thoughts to drift, attempting to get through the musicale with the least possible pain. His sister had taken him up with a vengeance on his offer to escort her to functions, he thought. He also suspected that Lord Brookfield had taken advantage of his offer to spend evenings at his club. So far his sacrifice had been for nothing, because he had not yet seen Anne and her cousin at any entertainments, except of course, the opera, where he could not approach them without seeming to single them out. Well, the Season had just begun, and perhaps Anne did not have access to circles as exalted as the one he and his sister moved in. He had made it his business to find out who the couple were whose box Anne and Miss Amberly had been in at the opera. Military family, of course. He should have known that would be the avenue by which Anne would try to enter Society.

Lord Stanton's hands clenched involuntarily as the soprano performing hit a particularly high and off-key note. The Season was not turning out to be as entertaining as he had hoped. It was quite the opposite, in fact, despite the company of Lady Parnell. Most of his set were still in Brighton with Prinny, and the enjoyment he had anticipated from watching Anne and her ward striving to be accepted in Society had not materialised. Perhaps he should use his influence to have Anne and Miss Amberly invited to some affairs in the upper echelons of Society. He debated whether it would constitute interfering with the terms of the bet. No, he decided, because it would benefit Anne, not hinder her. Although it would mean letting his sister guess about his interest in them.

The singer finished, and Lord Stanton applauded politely before turning to his sister.

"When are you holding your first entertainment this Season?" he asked.

"You *are* interested in the Season, aren't you?" Lady Brookfield replied, smoothing her mauve silk gown. "I was planning a ball for this next week."

"There is someone I would like you to invite."

Lady Brookfield's dark eyes showed interest. Perhaps at last she was going to find out who the mysterious woman was who had brought Harry to London so early. So far she had not been able to figure it out. There was Lady Parnell, of course, but she did not think it was she.

"Who?" she asked.

"Two people, actually. Miss Amberly and Miss Southwell."

Lady Brookfield recalled meeting both of them at a small rout party she had attended. Miss Amberly, of course, was one of the Season's new Incomparables, but she had difficulty placing Miss Southwell. It must be Miss Amberly Harry was interested in, which was surprising, since she was so young.

"I have met them," she said aloud. "If you will give me their direction I will see that they receive an invitation."

"I believe you should also include her sponsors, Colonel Halcott and his wife."

"Of course," she replied, determining to observe the two women very closely the next time she saw them. This was the first time Harry had made such a request of her. There had to be a reason.

Satisfied, Lord Stanton prepared to listen to the next performer with fortitude.

MRS. HALCOTT was somewhat surprised when they received their invitations to Lady Brookfield's ball.

"It is really something of a *coup*, my dear," she said to Anne as they rode in their carriage the night of the ball. "Invitations to Lady Brookfield's entertainments are much sought after. I wonder why she included us? Perhaps she noticed Melissa's beauty and invited us so the young gentlemen would have their Toast."

"I'm sure I don't know," Anne replied. "I don't even recall meeting Lady Brookfield, do you, Melissa?"

"No, although I have heard her name before," Melissa answered.

Whatever her reason for inviting them, Anne found that Lord and Lady Brookfield welcomed them most graciously and genuinely. Lord Brookfield was a handsome man of middle age who looked somewhat uncomfortable in his full evening dress. Anne felt he would be more at home among the sporting set or at his club. Lady Brookfield, in contrast, appeared to be in her element. She was exquisitely gowned in white satin lavishly embroidered in violet and wore a magnificent necklace of diamonds. Her dark good looks seemed somehow familiar to Anne, but she decided that she must have remembered her from other entertainments, choosing not to dwell upon it.

Lady Brookfield's ball was quite the most elaborate ball she had yet attended. Lady Brookfield had lavishly decorated the large yellow-and-white ballroom in the Oriental fashion. Eastern draperies were hung upon the walls, and exotic ornaments of brass had been placed about the room. The servants were all dressed in brightly coloured Oriental costumes, which made Anne feel as if she had just stepped into Turkey.

There was a great crush of people, most of them unknown to Anne and Melissa, although there were a few familiar faces. Lord Millbank was in attendance, as were Lady Conliffe and Viscount Woolbridge. Mrs. Halcott pointed out several people whose names they had often heard, but whom they had never seen. Lady Sefton and Mrs. Drummond-Burrel, two of the patronesses of Almack's, were present, as was the famous political hostess, Lady Melbourne. Anne thought the two patronesses looked very haughty and superior. She was glad she did not have to worry about being approved by them in order to gain entrance to Almack's. Lady Melbourne, on the other hand, appeared quite charming and approachable.

The guest Anne and Melissa were most interested in, however, was Beau Brummel, the arbiter of men's fashion. Anne could see why his word was law, for his sartorial style was faultless. He was clad in a perfectly fitting blue coat, white waistcoat, tight black breeches, striped silk stockings and a cravat that was an absolute marvel of starch and intricate folds. He was not dancing, but held court with a circle of admirers that included most of the fashionable gentlemen present. Having heard many tales of his sharp wit, they were just as glad there was little likelihood of being presented to him.

Melissa was soon swept away to the dance floor by Lord Woolbridge. Anne, elegant in gold velvet, did not lack for a partner long. Lord Millbank minced up to her and, bowing carefully so as not to disarrange his attire, solicited her hand for the boulanger. He was dressed all-the-crack in a purple coat with velvet collar, canary waistcoat, high stock, shirt points up to his ears and a huge ruby shirt broach. Anne accepted, wondering why the young sprig of fashion sought her out. She would have thought one of the young girls in their first Season would be a better partner than she. The earl danced well, if cautiously, and his notice of her moved several other men to request dances. As the evening progressed, many gentlemen she had not met before asked to be presented, and she had no forewarning when she heard her hostess's voice behind her.

"Miss Southwell, another gentleman has requested that I make him known to you."

Anne turned with a gracious smile upon her face, which froze upon her lips. For the first time since she had left Longworth she found herself face-to-face with Lord Henry Stanton. He was more handsome than she had remembered, and rivalled the Beau in his tight-fitting olive green coat, cream waistcoat, drab-coloured kerseymere breeches and perfectly tied cravat.

"May I present Lord Henry Stanton, Marquess of Talford. And also," Lady Brookfield added with a smile, "my brother."

She looked curiously at Anne, watching her reaction to her brother. Although she had thought he knew Miss Southwell, he had asked her to present him. Yet the look on Miss Southwell's face seemed to indicate that she already knew him. Perhaps she had heard of his reputation.

"My Lord," Anne faltered. Lady Brookfield was his sister. That explained why she had seemed familiar.

"I am at your service," Lord Stanton replied, lifting her hand to his lips, most improperly, since Anne was unmarried. "May I have the pleasure of this dance?" he continued.

Anne accepted, if somewhat hesitantly, and Lord Stanton led her out for the quadrille. As their fingers touched, Anne once again felt the thrill that seemed to invade her very being, and she pulled back almost imperceptibly.

"There is no danger to your reputation in being presented to me at my sister's," he assured her, mistaking the reason for her hesitation.

"I didn't realize Lady Brookfield was your sister," Anne said, trying to collect herself. A new thought occurred to her. "You had something to do with us being invited here, didn't you?" she accused.

"I confess. But I am not hindering your chances of winning the bet. To be seen at my sister's can only enhance your credit."

"Perhaps," Anne agreed, before the steps of the dance separated them.

When they came back together, Lord Stanton continued, "It seems you were doing quite well without my assistance, however. I see the rumours of Lord

Woolbridge's interest in your cousin are based on fact.'' He nodded towards the couple dancing not far from them.

Anne could not help the look of satisfaction that came over her features as she looked in the direction of his nod.

''Yes, Viscount Woolbridge has shown a marked preference for Melissa.''

She was unable to say more as the dance came to an end and Lord Stanton escorted her off the floor. He offered to procure her a glass of lemonade, and Anne accepted gratefully. When he returned, he found Anne gazing at the corner of the ballroom where Brummel was still holding court.

''I see you are interested in the Beau,'' he commented. ''Would you like to be presented to him?''

''You are acquainted with Beau Brummel?'' Anne asked, and then answered her own question. ''Of course, he is an intimate of the Prince also. But I don't think I care to meet him. I've heard too many tales of his cutting wit. I don't wish him to sharpen it on my provincial self.''

''I don't think you would give him cause,'' said Lord Stanton, looking at her with admiration. ''In any case, he is not always as cruel as he is made out to be. You would not believe it, but he has his soft spots. For instance, he is quite fond of animals, even mice.''

Anne looked at Lord Stanton dubiously, thinking he was making a May-game of her. She could not imagine the superior-looking Beau liking mice. She wanted to pursue the conversation, but was unable to as her next partner came toward her to claim his dance. Lord Stanton also looked disappointed at having their conversation disrupted.

"I hope we shall see each other more often, Miss Southwell," he said. "I should like to keep a closer watch on the progress of my wager."

Anne felt a rush of pleasure at the thought of seeing him more often, but she simply thanked him for the dance and the lemonade before turning to her next partner. As he walked away she felt strangely bereft, although she smiled pleasantly at Mr. Spencer, who was waiting patiently for her attention.

When Mr. Spencer returned Anne to her place by Mrs. Halcott, that lady took Anne to task for her dance with Lord Stanton.

"Oh, my dear," she said, "how could Lady Brookfield present you to Lord Stanton? Although," she added, "I don't suppose she could refuse, since he is her brother. But you really should not have talked to him so long. It will cause comment. And you must refuse any other dances."

"Don't worry, Mrs. Halcott," Anne reassured her friend. "I don't think he will approach me for another, and if he does I shall make my excuses."

"At least it was you and not Melissa," Mrs. Halcott went on, "I don't suppose one dance will be much remarked upon."

Anne agreed, and her warning delivered, Mrs. Halcott left Anne a moment to go speak to a friend she spied across the room.

Anne was waiting for her next partner to claim his dance when she was surprised to be approached by Lady Conliffe, elegant in a thin yellow muslin laced with diamond chains. It outlined her slender figure spectacularly, and Anne couldn't help thinking uncharitably that she must have been aware of it.

"I see you are ignoring my advice about Lord Stanton, Miss Southwell," she said in a cool voice. "Lord Stanton rarely dances with unmarried women. To be so singled out by him will do your reputation no good. Or your cousin's," she added with a malicious edge to her voice, looking to where Lord Woolbridge was standing with Melissa as she waited for the next gentleman to claim his dance.

"I could hardly refuse a partner my hostess presented me with, Lady Conliffe," Anne responded levelly.

"Then you have not met Lord Stanton before?"

"No indeed. Until this night I have endeavoured to follow your advice most scrupulously," Anne replied mendaciously, not wishing to antagonize the girl, no matter how she disliked her.

Lady Conliffe looked at Anne sharply, and left her with a cool nod, leaving Anne feeling uneasy. Lady Conliffe seemed to suspect some connexion between herself and Lord Stanton, although she knew it was quite impossible that she knew anything of their former acquaintance. Still, she sensed the girl's strong antagonism and knew it would not do to underestimate her. Anne had taken Captain Leslie's warning to heart, particularly since she had found out that Lady Conliffe had been expecting Lord Woolbridge to offer for her before he transferred his affections to Melissa. Well, there was little she could do about it at the moment. She resolved to remain on guard where Lady Conliffe was concerned.

If she had been able to read Lady Conliffe's mind she would have been less happy. Lady Conliffe was very angry indeed, and when Lord Woolbridge took Melissa into supper instead of her, she determined to do something to destroy their chances in Society. An opportunity was not long in presenting itself. While she and Miss Spencer waited for their supper partners to bring their plates, the conversation turned to Miss Amberly and Miss Southwell.

"Miss Amberly is so beautiful. I shall be glad when she accepts an offer and releases her court to the rest of us," sighed Miss Spencer, the rather plain daughter of a baron. She looked rather wistfully at the table where Melissa sat with Lord Woolbridge.

"Yes, it does appear that she has succeeded in her aims," Lady Conliffe replied.

"What do you mean, Lady Conliffe?"

"Oh, didn't you know?" Lady Conliffe lowered her voice confidentially. "Miss Amberly's father was quite all-to-pieces when he died, and her only hope to escape the poorhouse is to make a good match."

"Really? They don't appear to be poor. They have beautiful clothes, and I believe they reside in Mayfair."

"Yes, it is very brave of them to use all they have in a last attempt to recoup by making a good match," Lady Conliffe said, shaking her head in apparent sympathy.

Miss Spencer looked at Miss Amberly in disbelief—Lady Conliffe sat back, satisfied. She had achieved her goal without appearing spiteful. Let the rumours do their work.

Lord Stanton had hoped to escape his sister's ball before being cornered by her, but reckoned without her foresight. As he waited to have his carriage brought round, he was joined in the hall by Lady Brookfield.

"Oh, no, you don't, Harry. I thought you would try to escape early, and instructed the servants to notify me when you called for your carriage."

Lord Stanton gave in gracefully.

"My dear sister, I didn't know you were so fond of my company."

"You know quite well what I wish to discuss with you. Your carriage is not being brought round. Kindly wait for me in the library until my guests have departed," she commanded, leaving the hall in a swish of silk.

Lord Stanton went up the stairs to his brother-in-law's well-stocked library and, settling in a comfortable wing chair with a book, waited for his sister to join him.

It was quite two hours later before his sister, looking very tired, came in and sank gratefully onto a sofa.

"Thank goodness that's over. I am getting too old to hold such entertainments."

"You know you enjoy it, Caroline. Get on with your questions so I can go to my rooms and sleep," Lord Stanton directed, laying his book down on the Pembroke table beside him.

"To Lady Parnell's rooms, more likely, since Lord Parnell is not in Town. Now, be honest, Harry. What do you have to do with Miss Amberly and Miss Southwell? They are both beauties, I grant you, but not in your style. Miss Amberly is much too young, and Miss Southwell does not have the town bronze you prefer."

"Do you know my taste that well? But you are correct," he agreed untruthfully. "This time my interest is quite innocent, even praiseworthy. I simply wished to help Miss Amberly and Miss Southwell become established in Society. I was acquainted with Miss Southwell's brother before he was killed in Egypt."

"What do you take me for, a complete flat?" asked Lady Caroline, removing her slippers and tucking her feet under her skirts. "You've never associated with military men, and I've yet to know you to do something out of the kindness of your heart. For women, that is," she amended.

"Believe what you wish, Caro. The fact remains that I do have an interest in seeing how they get along this Season, and I do not wish to attract undesirable attention to them by interfering myself."

Lady Brookfield observed her brother meditatively a few moments. He was exhibiting one of the least appealing aspects of his personality. She knew he was not being honest with her, and was convinced he was up to no good as far as Miss Southwell and Miss Amberly were concerned. It *was* most unlike him to have anything to do with respectable unmarried women. Well, she would watch out for Miss Amberly and Miss Southwell herself.

Lord Stanton scowled blackly at his sister, angry at her for activating his conscience. Seeing Anne tonight had increased his desire to possess her, but his sister's words reminded him that what he planned was in fact quite reprehensible.

Lady Brookfield noted his scowl and, knowing that she would get nothing more out of him that night, changed the subject.

Lord Stanton made his escape as quickly as he could, directing his carriage to Lady Parnell's. Halfway there, the thought that his sister suspected where he was going made the intended end to his evening unpalatable, and he shouted at his driver to take him home instead. He went into his rooms in a foul temper, and without waiting for his valet, he tore off his clothes, throwing them about the room as he prepared to go to bed alone. When Lewis came in a short time later, he viewed the torn and scattered clothes with dismay, but picked them up quietly. He knew better than to make any comments when his master was in a temper.

AT HER HOUSE on Half Moon Street that night, Anne lay awake in a mood of exultation. The minor problems she had had were overcome. Thanks to the sponsorship of Colonel and Mrs. Halcott, the doors of Society had opened to them, and now with their appearance at one of Lady Brookfield's entertainments their place in Society was assured.

Anne's brow creased momentarily in puzzlement as she realised again that they must owe Lady Brookfield's invitation to Lord Stanton. She stared thoughtfully at the night shadows the raised plasterwork design cast on the ceiling as she tried to understand Lord Stanton's motive in having them invited to his sister's. Why was he aiding her to establish her ward in Society? Was it really his sense of fair play? Or did he perhaps regret the wager, and this was his way of helping her win so she would not have to pay? If that was the case, she would have to return the money later, to satisfy *her* sense of fair play. But that, she thought with satisfaction, would be simple, the way things were going.

Her thoughts turned to her ward. Melissa's debut in Society had been quite as successful as she could have hoped. Melissa's sweet nature and charming conduct were such that even the sourest of the ton ladies had found nothing to dislike in her manners. The gentlemen appeared to be captivated by Melissa, and several of the nobility had already shown an interest in her, the foremost amongst whom was Lord Woolbridge. Yes, whether Lord Stanton held her to it or not, the wager was hers.

The excitement of her success kept Anne awake a long time, but she finally fell asleep, where visions of her triumph invaded even her sleeping thoughts. She dreamed of Melissa, radiant in a wedding gown of cerulean blue, going down the aisle of the cathedral in view of all the ton to stand by the side of Viscount Woolbridge.

THE FOLLOWING MORNING, Lady Amelia called to talk with Melissa about the previous evening's ball.

"I wish Mama had planned to have my come-out earlier so I could be attending more entertainments," she said wistfully.

"Could you go to Vauxhall?" asked Melissa. "I have been wanting to go there this age, but haven't been able to persuade Anne to get up a party."

"Oh, yes," Lady Amelia said excitedly, "do let us go. There would be nothing to object to my going there before my ball."

Anne hesitated, knowing that the Gardens were a place where the lower classes mixed freely with the gentry, and that there were things that went on that young girls should not see. She had an unexpected ally in Lord Millbank, who had accompanied his sister on her call.

"You may certainly not go to Vauxhall, 'Melia. I won't escort you. Too fatiguing, don't you know," he said in his most bored voice, flicking his new enamel-glass snuffbox open languidly and taking a pinch.

Anne smiled, thinking that although Lord Millbank tried very hard to cultivate his attitudes, she felt sure that underneath the outrageous clothes and mannerisms was a nice young man.

"Oh, George," protested his sister, "do let us go. May we go if we find someone else to escort us? I am so bored with not being allowed to go anywhere until I have my ball."

"Yes, please, Anne," Melissa added her importunings. "I am certain Lieutenant Halcott and Captain Leslie would escort us. We would be safe with them."

"Suppose that would be well enough," Lord Millbank agreed.

Anne weakened. She wished to see the Gardens herself.

"You may go if Mrs. Halcott agrees it is an acceptable outing," she said encouragingly.

"Oh, thank you," Melissa exclaimed, and the two girls began to make plans excitedly. Lord Millbank turned his conversation with Anne back to the more interesting subject of his tailor, and the time passed pleasantly until their half-hour was up.

WHEN THEIR PARTY ARRIVED at Vauxhall three evenings later, Anne was glad that Melissa had prevailed on her to agree to the outing. In addition to the Halcotts, Captain Leslie, and Lady Amelia, Mr. and Miss Spencer had agreed to go, and it was a very convivial party that set out. Vauxhall was a beautiful place. Luxuriant shrubs and trees lined the walks, and beautiful flowers bloomed in profusion. They could hear music coming from the orchestra pavilion, and were fascinated by the variety of people they passed on the walks. Captain Leslie conducted them to the box where they were to eat their supper, and Anne was pleased to see that it abutted on the promenade so they could watch the people passing by. They dined on the specialties of Vauxhall, powdered beef and delicate custard laced with wine.

After supper the temptation to investigate the walks was irresistible. Major Halcott preferred to stay in their box enjoying his Arrack punch, but Mrs. Halcott gave her permission for the younger members of the party to explore, as long as they did not go into the Dark Walks. They started on their explorations together, but soon Anne and Captain Leslie became separated from the younger couples. Anne wished to see the famous statue of Handel by Roubiliac, while the younger people were more interested in visiting the dancing pavilion. They walked slowly down the tree-lined avenue leading to the statue, admiring the waterfalls and fountains. As they started on their way back to the box, Captain Leslie teased Anne.

"Would you dare brave Mrs. Halcott's wrath to go into the Dark Walks with me?"

"Why not? I think I would be quite safe with you," said Anne, smiling at Captain Leslie and looking meaningfully at the sword by his side.

"I don't think it was only the dangers from inebriated young bucks and commoners Mrs. Halcott was worried about," responded Captain Leslie, taking Anne's arm.

As they went into the famous Dark Walks, Anne was very grateful for the captain's presence, for the walks *were* dark, and they passed several unsavoury-looking characters who leered menacingly at Anne, although no one dared more with her officer escort by her side. As they got deeper into the walks they also passed several couples who looked as though they would rather not have been disturbed. They came into a quiet spot by a grotto, where Captain Leslie stopped and took Anne's hands in his.

"Anne," he said softly, bending to place a soft kiss upon her lips.

Captain Leslie's kiss was warm and pleasurable, but Anne did not feel the sensations she had felt when Lord Stanton kissed her at Longworth. Had that kiss been an exception, she wondered, brought about by her fatigue and the port? Would she feel the same for a kiss from Captain Leslie under similar circumstances?

Captain Leslie did not seem to find anything lacking in her response, and he held her hand tightly as they started back out of the Dark Walks. When they arrived back at their box, it was to find the others already returned. Mrs. Halcott looked at them closely. Anne couldn't help feeling a little self-conscious, knowing she suspected where they had been. She said nothing, however, and Anne decided that Mrs. Halcott trusted her to behave circumspectly. They joined the others in having more refreshments while they waited for the fireworks display. Later when the behaviour of the people in the gardens began to deteriorate noticeably, Mrs. Halcott declared they had stayed long enough, and the party went home, very satisfied with their outing.

VAUXHALL PROVED TO BE the last outing Anne could enjoy whole-heartedly, for she soon began to notice that their invitations were falling off, evidently since the ball at Lady Brookfield's. Melissa, still inundated with requests to go riding and walking with young gentlemen, and happy in her friendship with Lady Amelia, did not seem to notice, but Anne did, and began to worry. She found it had not been her imagination one day when Mrs. Halcott made an early morning call.

"I am glad to find you by yourself," Mrs. Halcott said when Anne told her that Melissa was out driving with Lord Woolbridge. "There is something I wish to discuss." She stopped a moment to take a sip of tea.

"There are some distressing rumours going around. Nothing too bad," she hastened to reassure Anne at her expression of alarm, "but we must do something to counteract them. It's being put about that you and Melissa are penniless, and are attempting to foist yourself off on the ton in an endeavour to make good matches."

Anne was hard put not to laugh. "But Mrs. Halcott," she protested, "many of the members of the ton have little money and attempt to recoup by making good matches. I don't see how such talk can affect one of Melissa's beauty and good nature. Although," she added slowly, "I have noticed that our invitations have been fewer since the ball at Lady Brookfield's."

Mrs. Halcott nodded. "You see. If you and Melissa were better known in Society, or if you had higher ranks, such talk would not affect you at all. But the two of you have suddenly appeared upon the scene, and stolen much attention from other girls making their come-outs. There are many who were looking for a reason to exclude you, and even such a minor thing is enough. It doesn't help that Melissa's father *was* pretty much all-to-pieces when he died. Not that it's

Melissa's fault that her father made some unwise investments, but there you are."

She shook her head sadly at the improvidence of Melissa's parents in leaving their daughter unprovided for.

"However, you're not to worry. I've done what I could to counteract the rumours. You told me that Melissa did have a dowry, which I've implied is fairly substantial."

"Melissa's dowry *is* fairly substantial," Anne agreed cautiously, "but I would not wish to mislead people."

"Oh, no, my dear, I have not specified an amount; I've simply assured those who have inquired that it does exist. The rest they do for me," she concluded.

Anne looked at Mrs. Halcott in some dismay. If word got back to Lord Stanton, would he consider that she had forfeited the wager? She was not supposed to mention the amount of Melissa's dowry, but Mrs. Halcott had said she did not specify an amount. Certainly she could not fault Mrs. Halcott. She could have had no way of knowing.

"Thank you for telling me about the rumours and what you have been doing to stop them," Anne said, "but I would prefer not to emphasise Melissa's dowry. It is not that substantial."

"Now don't you worry," Mrs. Halcott said, patting Anne's hand fondly. "Melissa will make a fine match before the Season is over. With her charm and beauty we will be able to ride out this small setback."

After Mrs. Halcott left, Anne poured another cup of the now cold tea and pondered the ways of Society. It still seemed unbelievable that a rumour that she and Melissa had no money could do much damage. Perhaps it was because they *appeared* to have money, she decided. They resided at a good address and wore fashionable clothes. She supposed the ton would look upon that as an intentional deception, since they were newcomers in Society. Upstarts trying to enter where they had no right to be. Fortunately, except for the fewer invitations, they did not seem to have lost by the rumours. Viscount Woolbridge still called upon them, as did others of Melissa's admirers. She leaned forward to pour another cup of tea, spilling half of it into the saucer when Benton announced another caller.

"Lord Stanton."

CHAPTER SEVEN

ANNE SET DOWN the Staffordshire teapot with an unsteady hand and rose to greet Lord Stanton. Despite her shock at seeing him, she could not help being amused by the expression on her butler's face. It was a comical combination of awe, admiration, concern and pugnacity. The confident manners and the exquisite tailoring of the marquess's clothes demanded Benton's veneration, but he was also aware of Lord Stanton's less than savoury reputation. He could not refuse to announce him, but he was concerned about leaving him in the drawing room alone with his mistress. Anne reassured Benton with a nod.

"Please bring some refreshment for Lord Stanton, Benton."

"Where did you get that butler?" Lord Stanton asked as Benton left the room. "He is still wet behind the ears."

"That's one way we cut down on expenses," explained Anne. "He gives very good service despite his youth," she said in his defense.

Anne sat down on the damask sofa, while Lord Stanton lounged negligently against the mantelpiece, looking about the modestly furnished room.

"Why are you here, singling me out, Lord Stanton?" Anne asked after Benton had served Lord Stanton with wine and left them alone. "You are not keeping to the terms of the wager."

"I, Miss Southwell?" countered Lord Stanton. "You, I believe, were the first to digress, spreading about word of your cousin's dowry."

"Indeed I did not, my lord," Anne said, much stung. "I have said nothing about Melissa's dowry. Mrs. Halcott was questioned by the mamas of some of Melissa's prospective suitors, and only assured them that Melissa *had* a dowry. Mrs. Halcott told me that there is a rumour going about that Melissa and I are penniless, and she was afraid it might hurt Melissa's chances of making a good match."

Lord Stanton observed Anne's heightened colour and angry green eyes, thinking again how beautiful and desirable she was. He admired the picture she made in her long-sleeved pink muslin morning dress and lace cap, wishing he could remove the cap and run his fingers through her hair.

An impatient shake of Anne's head recalled him to his reasons for stopping at Half Moon Street. He was aware of the rumours of their insolvency as well as the counter-rumours about the dowry. He had supposed the temptation to tell of the dowry when the rumours of their financial state began had compelled Anne to act impulsively. Seeing her, he knew that not even the rumours would have moved her not to play fairly.

"Very well, I will accept your word, if you in turn will forgive my calling upon you here," he said, leaving his position by the fireplace and seating himself across from Anne on a mahogany Chippendale-style chair.

"Gladly, Lord Stanton. I concede that you thought you had cause to take me to task," Anne acknowledged.

"Let us cry pax, then," Lord Stanton said with the smile Anne found so irresistible. "Perhaps I can even help you," he added. "Do you have any idea where the rumours of your precarious financial state originated?"

"None at all, Lord Stanton," Anne said, shaking her head in bewilderment. "It could have been anyone who knew of the baronet's financial state when he died. I confess, I have been having difficulty believing that such an insignificant rumour could so affect our social life. Many of the girls making their come-outs this Season do not have great fortunes."

"I did warn you not to make wagers about things of which you had insufficient knowledge," reminded Lord Stanton. "Society is rarely kind, or fair. Even my title and wealth do not admit me to Almack's or to the homes of some of the highest sticklers."

"In your case I think it is warranted," Anne replied with spirit.

"Perhaps I have reformed," he suggested.

"Lord Parnell would not agree," Anne replied, and then blushed at the indelicacy of her response.

Lord Stanton, however, merely grinned. "Jealous? There is no reason to be, I assure you."

Anne blushed more deeply, again feeling the pull of Lord Stanton's personality. The intimacy she had felt with him at Longworth had been subtly re-established. They sat for a moment in silence, each very aware of the other. Anne was not sure whether to be glad or sorry when Sanders came in with some needlework and settled herself in a corner chair. Evidently, Benton, worried about his mistress's reputation, had informed Sanders of Lord Stanton's call.

Lord Stanton smiled wryly at Anne, and finishing his wine, he rose to leave. As he was bidding Anne good-bye, Melissa and Lord Woolbridge returned. Lord Woolbridge could not conceal a look of surprise at Lord Stanton's presence in the drawing room, but he greeted him civilly. Melissa greeted him with more warmth, asking him to stay, but the marquess begged another appointment and departed.

As Anne rang for more refreshments, two more callers were announced, and Lord Millbank and his sister entered the room. Anne smiled to herself. The rumours hadn't scared off their closest friends—that was evident by the parade of company they were having this morning. As was becoming usual, Lord Millbank attached himself to Anne. He was dressed in the latest stare of fashion in a wasp-waisted coat with puffed shoulders, two waistcoats of different lengths and colours, and striped trousers. Anne was beginning to puzzle over Lord Millbank's attention to her, not realizing that her beauty and the polite consideration she gave to his questions of dress were a compelling attraction. Younger women were too concerned with their own appearance to give his proper attention, in Lord Millbank's experience.

As Lord Millbank expounded on the merits of Scheltz versus Weston, Anne intercepted a wistful look Lady Amelia directed at Lord Woolbridge and Melissa as the two conversed. Anne wondered how Lady Amelia would take when she was presented, and feared she would not be a great success despite her connexions. Her manners, though pleasing, were too quiet, and her looks were only passable. Anne tried to think of some single young gentleman who might find Lady Amelia attractive, but she came up empty-handed. It was an unfortunate fact that gentlemen as a rule did not appreciate the qualities of a shy young girl like Lady Amelia. Anne realised she was trying to matchmake, and decided she should not interfere.

After their guests left, Melissa spoke to Anne.

"Why did Lord Stanton come here this morning, Anne? I thought he was going to avoid us to protect our reputations. Does he feel it is safe for us to be friends now?"

"He wished to find out how we were getting along, and felt it would be safe for him to make a short morning call," Anne said evasively, glancing at Sanders, still sitting in the corner with her sewing.

"That was thoughtful of him. I do like Lord Stanton. It is a pity he has such a bad reputation." Melissa was silent for a moment, then asked, "Anne, what do you think of Captain Leslie?"

"Captain Leslie?" Anne repeated, her thoughts still with Lord Stanton.

"Yes. I noticed his behaviour towards you the night we went to Vauxhall, and I think he is becoming quite fond of you. If he makes an offer, will you accept?"

Anne thought a moment before answering. Would she accept? She liked and respected Captain Leslie—the talks she had had with him about her father and brother had been cleansing—but did she have the feelings for him that a woman should for a man she wished to marry? Anne didn't think so, remembering the kiss at Vauxhall.

"I don't know, Melissa. I really hadn't thought about marrying, myself. How do you feel about *your* most persistent suitors, Lord Woolbridge and Lieutenant Halcott? They appear to be laying claim to you at the functions we've attended, and are frightening away any other prospective suitors with their black looks."

Anne did not really think Melissa considered young Lieutenant Halcott a serious suitor, but the rivalry that had been developing between him and Lord Woolbridge was most amusing. Melissa laughed, accepting Anne's change of subject.

"It's too early to decide. They are both very agreeable, but so are most of the gentlemen I've met. I don't know."

That evening they attended a minor ball given at the small brick-fronted town house of Mrs. Spencer's sister, Mrs. Chambers. Anne entered the house with some trepidation, wondering if they would be cut by any of those attending who had heard the rumours about their financial state. However, Mr. and Mrs. Chambers welcomed them courteously, and as she and Melissa were shown into the double drawing rooms which had been opened out to form a ballroom, she was relieved to find they were greeted as usual by their acquaintances.

Melissa was quickly surrounded by her court, with Viscount Woolbridge and Lieutenant Halcott most prominent. Evidently, whatever damage had been done by the rumours of their insolvency had been counteracted by the stories of Melissa's dowry put about by Mrs. Halcott, or many of her admirers would have deserted her. Anne gave a sigh of relief as the first set began to form, and was once again grateful for such a friend as Mrs. Halcott.

Anne would not have felt as secure if she had observed Lady Conliffe's face at that moment. Lady Conliffe had not intended to put in an appearance at Mrs. Chambers's ball, as it was not a particularly fashionable gathering. Earlier that week, though, she had spoken to Lord Woolbridge at a rout. He had asked if she would be attending the Chambers' ball, and had solicited her hand for the opening dance. Lord Woolbridge had been spending more and more time with Miss Amberly and correspondingly less with her, so Lady Conliffe thought it politic to say she would be at the ball.

Hoping to recapture Lord Woolbridge's straying attention, Lady Conliffe had dressed with especial care for the evening, and knew she was looking her best. She wore a peach print muslin gown of exceptionally fine material that exhibited her tall and slender form to advantage. She had accentuated the fashionable square décolletage of her gown with a simple diamond pendant, and the diamond drops hanging from her delicate ears drew attention to her graceful throat. Perfectly fitting gloves of peach silk emphasized her shapely arms, and a headdress of peach and white flowers tied with silk ribbands adorned her glossy dark hair. She had received many admiring looks from both the ladies and the gentlemen present, but Lord Woolbridge, who had not even noticed her, was leading Miss Amberly out for the first set!

None of Lady Conliffe's fury at the unforgivable snub Lord Woolbridge was dealing her showed on her face as she stood alone for a moment as the men led out their partners for the opening set. A young man soon noticed her partnerless state and, not believing his good fortune, hastened to request Lady Conliffe's hand for the dance.

Lady Conliffe smiled graciously and accepted, but as she automatically performed the steps of the dance, she could not help directing several dagger glances towards Miss Amberly. That provincial chit! She looked hardly old enough to be at a ball, in her unfashionably full-skirted muslin gown trimmed with blue ribbands and bows.

The figures of the dance brought Lady Conliffe and her partner close to Lord Woolbridge and Miss Amberly, and she had the satisfaction of seeing Lord Woolbridge stumble and turn fiery red as the realisation of what he had done came over him.

After the dance, Lady Conliffe's eager young partner went to procure a glass of ratafia for her, and she saw a flustered Lord Woolbridge approaching her chair.

"Lady Conliffe, I—I—" he stuttered, all his usual social grace deserting him completely. Genuinely stricken by his appalling breach of manners, he searched his mind desperately for something to say that would rectify the situation.

"Yes?" Lady Conliffe asked sweetly, fanning herself lightly as though from the exertion of the dance, determined to offer no help to the miserable viscount. Let him get himself out of his coil. She looked at him coolly, her extreme anger betrayed only by two bright red spots on her cheeks and the audible snap with which she closed her painted silk fan.

Fortunately for Lord Woolbridge, Lady Conliffe's partner returned with her ratafia at this juncture. Lady Conliffe took it with a smile as the young man bowed to the viscount.

"Lord Woolbridge," he said, recognising Lady Conliffe's frequent escort, feeling proud of himself at having stolen a march on the lord.

"Sheldon." Lord Woolbridge nodded briefly and turned back to Lady Conliffe. "I wished to request the pleasure of your hand for the next dance," he said, unable to think of anything else to do.

"Thank you, but I have already promised the next set to Lord Atherby. It would be shockingly ill-mannered of me to dance with you when he has a prior claim," she said, smiling, showing her beautifully white and even teeth. "Perhaps another time."

"Yes, of course," Lord Woolbridge muttered, and with another nod to Mr. Sheldon, he went to join some friends, looking far from his usual debonair self.

Lady Conliffe went through the rest of the evening with a smile on her face, but she was seething inside. Miss Amberly would pay for the insult she had received this night, she and her cousin Miss Southwell. It did not matter to Lady Conliffe that the snub had been dealt by Lord Woolbridge, not Miss Amberly, nor that Miss Amberly could have had no knowledge of Lord Woolbridge's promise to dance the opening set with another. Her anger was all directed towards the girl who was the unwitting cause of the humiliation of having a gentleman forget he had promised a dance to her. She, Lady Conliffe, should be the *cause* of such snubs, not the recipient.

All though the evening, as she danced, and later as she ate her supper, Lady Conliffe tried to think of a way to destroy Miss Amberly and Miss Southwell for good in the eyes of Society. Rumours were the best way, of course, but the ones she had started about their precarious financial situation had not had the effect she'd hoped. She would have to think of something stronger.

The cousins were seated at a supper table not far from hers, and Lady Conliffe looked at Miss Amberly thoughtfully. Then her gaze moved to Miss Southwell, who was dressed attractively in striped lutestring. Her eyes stayed on Miss Southwell, and she bit her lower lip speculatively. It occurred to her that Miss Amberly's guardian seemed inordinately interested in that rake, Hell-born Harry.

She remembered how Miss Southwell had been staring at Lord Stanton in Hyde Park that day, the glances she had stolen towards his box at the opera and how she had danced with him at Lady Brookfield's. Perhaps such an interest in a rake indicated a propensity in Miss Southwell that she could exploit. No one knew anything of Miss Southwell's history. It should be a relatively simple matter to cast doubt on her past. Yes, she would hint that Miss Amberly's guardian was not as good as she should be. And she would begin some discreet investigations into the backgrounds of the cousins. She had been foolish not to have done so before.

The first genuine smile of the evening lit Lady Conliffe's face, causing her supper partner, Lord Atherby, to think he must be a wit indeed to bring such a smile to the face of the Incomparable Lady Conliffe.

LADY BROOKFIELD was one of the first to hear of the new rumours about Miss Southwell. Since her brother had asked her to invite Miss Amberly and Miss Southwell to her ball, she had watched their progress in Society with interest. When Lady Sefton mentioned them during a call she made on Lady Brookfield one morning, she was instantly alert.

"I remember you invited Miss Amberly and Miss Southwell to your ball," Lady Sefton said, sitting back on the comfortable Hepplewhite chair, prepared for a good gossip. "Are you aware of the latest *on dit* concerning them?"

Lady Brookfield confessed her ignorance, and Lady Sefton was pleased to enlighten her. "I had it from a most reliable source that Miss Southwell is no better than she should be. Such a pity for Miss Amberly, for she is such a charming girl," she added with spurious sympathy.

Lady Brookfield laughed delightedly. "Wherever did you hear that? Nothing could be further from the truth," she assured Lady Sefton, although she was not quite sure it was *not* the truth. Perhaps that explained her brother's interest in Miss Southwell. Still, it would not do to have Miss Amberly's chances destroyed.

"I heard it from Lady Conliffe," Lady Sefton said, slightly indignant. "She had it from a woman who knew Miss Southwell in Brighton."

"Lady Conliffe," Lady Brookfield drawled. "Wasn't there talk of a match between her and Lord Woolbridge before he joined Miss Amberly's court? I wouldn't put much faith in her information."

Lady Sefton still appeared unconvinced, reluctant to give up such a juicy piece of gossip. Lady Brookfield deftly steered the conversation to other channels, determining to notify her brother of the rumours. If he had not already heard of them, he might wish to know. They could do serious damage.

As soon as Lady Sefton left, Lady Brookfield rang for her maid and went around to her brother's town house on St. James, but he was not at home. She left a note, telling him what she had heard and where the rumour had apparently originated.

LORD STANTON WAS AT BROOK'S, relaxing in a chair next to a blazing fire and reading a newspaper. He was perusing an interesting piece on Bonaparte's escalating activities on the Continent when he thought he heard Anne's name mentioned by some young bucks sitting on a sofa nearby.

"If that is true," one of them was saying, "then perhaps the Incomparable Miss Amberly would not be that difficult to approach. I wouldn't mind setting her up in a little house somewhere."

"I'd prefer her guardian," the first speaker said. "I like my women with a little more flesh."

Lord Stanton hesitated momentarily. He could not like allowing such a scurrilous remark to pass, but if a man of his reputation championed them it might bring more unwelcome speculation. A low remark followed by a coarse laugh decided him. He put down his newspaper and walked over to the sofa, standing in front of the low table. The young gentlemen looked up, surprised to be receiving attention from a nonesuch like Lord Stanton. They greeted him with a heartiness that quickly changed to uncertainty as they saw the cold glint in his eye. Lord Stanton addressed the first speaker.

"Sedgewick, could I have heard you impugning the honour of two ladies who shall remain nameless?" he asked, pulling off his gloves deliberately.

At the look of steel in Lord Stanton's eyes, any remaining bravado died in young Lord Sedgewick. Tales of early evening meetings at Primrose Hill and Hyde Park came to his mind.

"N—no, Lord Stanton, I am sure I would do no such thing," he stammered.

"I rather thought I had misunderstood you," Lord Stanton said, pulling his gloves back on. "I am glad to find that I was correct, for I would take it very ill to hear of any gently bred woman's reputation being slandered."

He inclined his head shortly to the two young men, who had both paled considerably.

"Good day, Sedgewick, Norton."

"My lord," Sedgewick said as Lord Stanton turned and walked away. He ran his fingers under his stock, which suddenly felt much too tight. He had the feeling he had had a very close call.

As Lord Stanton left the club and walked up the street, the irony of the situation hit him. He had been about to issue a challenge to a man, no, to a young cub, not to do the very thing *he* planned to do—destroy the reputation of Miss Southwell. It was no use telling himself that he would not do it so publicly—the end result would be the same.

What ailed him where the Southwell woman was concerned? He still desired her, and still intended to make her his mistress, but at the same time he had an urge to protect her. He strode along the street, swinging his walking stick with such a black scowl on his face that he unknowingly caused several passers-by to give him a wide berth.

He reached his town house and, after thrusting his top hat and stick at his footman, was handed two messages by his butler. One was from Prinny, who had arrived in London and wanted to see him. The other was from his sister. A thoughtful look came over his face as he read her note. So, Lady Conliffe was at the bottom of the rumour. Such a rumour could be far more damaging than the first, and more difficult to counteract. Why did it bother him, anyway? Wasn't this what he had wanted, what he had foreseen when he first made the wager with Anne? Then why did he have the desire to wring Lady Conliffe's slender neck? He sat in his study for a long time trying to figure out the answer before he remembered the summons from Prinny and set off for Carlton House.

ANNE DID NOT HEAR of the new rumours until that afternoon. Captain Leslie called and requested that Anne drive out with him in his phaeton. She was a little surprised, when, after handing her into the vehicle, he dismissed the groom, instructing him to wait until they returned. He drove into Hyde Park, and when they reached a relatively quiet area, he halted and addressed Anne.

"I wished to talk to you alone, Miss Southwell. I hope you do not think me presumptuous, but I believe you know that I take a sincere interest in your welfare and that of your ward."

"Yes, I know, Captain Leslie, and I appreciate your concern," Anne said, wondering what had brought such a serious expression to the man's face.

Captain Leslie was quiet a moment, as though he were not quite sure how to proceed.

"Are you aware, Miss Southwell, that there are rumours being spread about you?"

"Yes. Mrs. Halcott informed me that rumours were going about that we had no money, but they seemed to die quickly, and I have not noticed any ill effects from them."

"It is not that rumour, but a new one." Once again he hesitated, then plunged ahead. "The *on dit* now is that you are not quite what you should be."

Anne looked at him questioningly, and he appeared very uncomfortable.

"It is nothing concrete, which makes it all the harder to counteract. But I am afraid your behaviour is the basis for the gossip. It is being said that while Melissa is what she claims, you are not what you pretend to be, but an adventuress using Melissa's position to foist yourself upon the ton." As Anne sat in shocked silence, he continued. "I fear your seclusion these past years is giving credence to the story. Few people are acquainted with you or your family, and those who are are not of the highest ton."

Anne stared unhappily before her, not seeing the beauty of the Park.

"I am sorry to have distressed you," Captain Leslie said apologetically. "If it is any consolation to you, while this may close some of the doors of the ton to you, those who know you will continue to support you."

"Do you have any advice as to how I may counteract the rumours?"

"I am afraid there is little you can do but continue to appear at those social functions still open to you. In the end, a new *on dit* will take precedence and this will be forgotten."

Captain Leslie and Anne sat quietly as he drove slowly around the Park. After a few minutes he spoke again.

"This is not the time or place, Miss Southwell, but you must be aware of the regard in which I hold you. I had intended to speak later, but the circumstances lead me to show my hand earlier than I had intended. Please allow me to give you the protection of my name."

Anne moved as if to speak, but Captain Leslie waved her to silence. "Please, allow me to finish. Although I am not wealthy, we would live comfortably. I am the youngest son of a baron, but with five older brothers; I have no expectations of inheriting the title. Your cousin would be welcome in our home until she marries, which I am sure she will despite the gossip."

As Anne searched her mind for the appropriate response, Captain Leslie came to her rescue. "You need not think I require an answer right away. It would greatly please me if you would consider my offer, but I shall not press you. You have much to concern you and I am content to wait."

Anne smiled in gratitude but was nevertheless grateful when Captain Leslie turned the horses towards home.

ABOUT TWO HOURS after Anne left with Captain Leslie, Viscount Woolbridge called at Half Moon Street to ask if Melissa would care to go for a drive with him to Hyde Park. Melissa, who had been looking wistfully out the window at the fine day while she ostensibly worked at her embroidery, looked questioningly at Sanders, who nodded her head briefly.

Melissa went to fetch her parasol, gloves and pelisse and returned shortly with a happy smile of anticipation on her face. As she and Lord Woolbridge prepared to leave, she heard the front door, as Anne returned from her drive with Captain Leslie. Viscount Woolbridge, with his customary punctilious good manners, asked Anne to accompany them. Anne hesitated before answering, moving Melissa to add her plea.

"Please do come with us," she encouraged, not knowing that Anne's hesitation stemmed from the fact that while she didn't wish to go out driving again so soon, neither did she like to let Melissa go until she had been warned of the new rumours. "You are already dressed to go driving, and Lord Woolbridge's bays are such sweet goers."

Melissa blushed as the cant term slipped out, but her guardian didn't seem to notice.

"Thank you, Lord Woolbridge," Anne said, "I shall be pleased to accompany you and Melissa."

The footman, who had been standing nearby, handed Anne back her parasol and gloves, and the three went out to where the groom held the viscount's horses. Melissa thought her cousin looked rather serious as she was being handed into the glossy blue lacquered curricle, and wondered what had transpired on her drive with Captain Leslie. Well, a drive in the Park at the fashionable hour would restore her guardian's spirits.

Viscount Woolbridge was a skilled whip, and expertly maneuvered his team through the crush of vehicles in Hyde Park. He had not gone far when he encountered a large carriage with a crest emblazoned on the side. The viscount inclined his head deeply to the Dowager Duchess of Carroll, and she deigned to stop and speak to him.

Melissa had been presented to the Dowager Duchess of Carroll, and found her quite intimidating, and as the dowager finished speaking to the viscount, she looked up to her with a shy sweet smile, determined not to let her fear get in the way of her manners. But to Melissa's surprise, the dowager looked right past her and ordered her carriage to move one. She looked at Anne with surprise and hurt. Anne seemed unruffled by the dowager's cut, and she smiled at Melissa reassuringly.

Lord Woolbridge's normally open countenance appeared closed and angry as he flicked his team forward. He was too gentlemanly to refer to the cut directly, but he comforted Melissa as best he could.

"Her grace the Dowager Duchess of Carroll is exceedingly high in the instep. She thinks it below her to acknowledge anyone who does not have a title in their own right."

"Yes, and think what harm your reputation has been done in her eyes to be seen with the daughter of a baron, and worse, the daughter of a mere Major Southwell," Anne said lightly.

Melissa smiled uncertainly and tried to hide the hurt she had been dealt by the snub, but the jaunty angle at which she had held her parasol dropped. When Lord Woolbridge stopped his curricle to greet some more acquaintances, she shrank back imperceptibly into the squabs and did not look up until she was spoken to. However, the gentlemen were very courteous and complimentary to both Melissa and her cousin, and some of her confidence began to return. Lord Woolbridge smiled at her as though to say, "See!" and Anne squeezed her hand encouragingly.

As they continued around the Park and all the acquaintances they met spoke to them, Melissa's spirits recovered completely. Perhaps the dowager *was* simply high in the instep. She chatted happily with her friends, and noted the new fashions being exhibited by the people on the Promenade.

"Look at Miss Armstrong's bonnet," she said enviously to Anne as a curricle with that young woman and her mother came abreast of them. She looked longingly at the wide-brimmed bonnet of twist with a short lace veil.

Mrs. Armstrong exchanged greetings with the viscount and Melissa called cheerfully to her friend.

"Good afternoon, Mrs. Armstrong. Where did you purchase your new bonnet, Miss Armstrong? It becomes you wonderfully well."

To Melissa's consternation, Miss Armstrong did not reply to her question, but looked down to the floor of the curricle, and Mrs. Armstrong acted as though Melissa and her guardian were not even there. She looked to Anne and saw that her guardian was in her turn behaving as though no one were in the curricle next to theirs, holding herself proudly and speaking only to Lord Woolbridge. Melissa felt she should follow her guardian's example, but the unkind snub made her want to shrink into herself, not hold herself proudly erect.

The viscount put his curricle in motion without another glance or word to the Armstrongs. As they continued around the Park, Melissa's eyes shone with unshed tears. No one could say that a plain Mrs. Armstrong was too high in the instep to acknowledge a baron's daughter, she thought miserably. Something was seriously wrong. She noted gratefully that Lord Woolbridge was taking them back home. Earlier that afternoon she had longed to go out, but now she just wanted to return to the safety of the house on Half Moon Street.

AS THE COUSINS ENTERED the house and handed their wraps to Sanders, Melissa looked at Anne questioningly, and Anne told her to go into the drawing room where they could talk. She watched her miserable ward with compassion. This was what Captain Leslie had warned her about. She wished she could have spared Melissa the experience. She could see that Melissa was deeply hurt. Although, Anne thought wryly, the cuts they had experienced were nothing to what they could expect in the future if the rumours became widespread. She followed her ward into the drawing room.

"What is it, Anne?" Melissa asked, her eyes still filled with tears. "Why were we cut by the Dowager Duchess of Carroll and Mrs. Armstrong?"

Anne drew Melissa down on the settee beside her.

"I am afraid there are rumours going around about us again."

"The ones about our finances?" Melissa questioned.

"No, they are much worse this time," Anne explained. "Someone is saying that I am no better than I should be."

Melissa looked shocked, startled out of her misery at the cuts for a moment. She knew her cousin's upbringing had been unconventional, but no one could say Anne was not proper.

"Who would say such a thing?" she asked in bewilderment.

"I don't know," Anne sighed. "I would have warned you, but I did not know myself until Captain Leslie informed me of them this afternoon." She looked gravely at her ward. "I must prepare you. The cuts we experienced this afternoon on the drive with Lord Woolbridge were mild compared to what we may expect in the future. Probably the viscount's presence spared us some today."

Melissa was silent for a moment, her fingers unconsciously pleating the material of her gown. The experience of being cut had hurt her deeply. If that was what they could expect when they went out, she would rather stay in.

"What can we do?" she finally asked.

"There is very little we can do, I'm afraid," Anne admitted. "But although we shall be excluded from many of the ton's entertainments for a while, our real friends will continue to invite us to theirs, and in time another *on dit* will take precedence over this one and it will be forgotten."

As soon as she said the words, Anne wondered if she had done the right thing to give Melissa too much hope. It was possible these rumours would not pass as quickly as the last. It was true that their friends would not desert them, but the question was how many friends they had. Well, even Captain Leslie had said it would pass with time. She hugged Melissa closely and, taking a handkerchief from her reticule, dried her ward's eyes.

"Don't worry, Melissa, it will come right in the end," she said. That at least she could say with confidence, Anne thought.

Melissa smiled and returned her guardian's hug. "I know it will," she replied with a quaver in her voice that belied the brave words.

NOT FAR AWAY, Lord Stanton relaxed with Prince George in Carlton House, the Prince's preferred residence when he was in Town. The Prince did not get along at all well with his father, particularly since the marriage George III had arranged for his son with the Princess Caroline. When in London, the Prince of Wales chose to live in his own palace, surrounded by his intimate friends. They sat together companionably, drinking some of the Prince's favourite cherry brandy.

"Enlighten me concerning the latest *on dits*," commanded the Prince. "What's this I hear about the latest Incomparable being chaperoned by a woman who's no better than she should be, eh? Miss Amberly, I think her name was. Never got to see her, and now it's unlikely she'll be attending many functions. Is she as beautiful as they say?"

Lord Stanton thought that perhaps here he would have a chance to aid Anne and Miss Amberly. He organized his thoughts carefully.

"Yes. It's a pity, for Miss Amberly is truly beautiful, and good as well. She and her cousin, who is her guardian, came to Town so she might have a chance to make a good match. The guardian, Miss Southwell, is the daughter of Major Southwell. He and his son were both killed in Egypt while serving under Abercromby. It's a pity the rumours are ruining their chances, for there's not a speck of truth to them."

"How'd they get started?"

Lord Stanton played his trump card. "Believe it was Lady Conliffe. One of her court, the Viscount Woolbridge, transferred his affections to Miss Amberly."

The Prince shifted his considerable bulk and his chair creaked. He glowered angrily at the mention of Lady Conliffe, for he disliked her intensely. Some cutting remarks she had made about his weight during the Season last year had been overheard and reported.

"By God, I won't have it, Stanton," the Prince said suddenly, lowering his glass of cherry brandy and banging his fist on the table. "Can't have the lives of daughters of our loyal officers being ruined by scurrilous lies."

"Perhaps if you were to invite them to a supper at Carlton House..." Lord Stanton suggested.

"Capital idea! If I am seen to notice them, all but the highest sticklers must accept them." The Prince looked at Lord Stanton shrewdly. "How d'ye come to know so much about them, Stanton? Didn't know you were interested in young misses."

"The older cousin is not a young miss, but a beautiful woman," said Lord Stanton.

"Oh, so that's the way the wind blows, is it? Well, I'll help you out Stanton," he agreed, and added under his breath, "particularly if it will serve Lady Conliffe a bad turn."

CHAPTER EIGHT

THE ARRIVAL OF THE THICK cream-coloured invitation with gold edges sent the whole household at Half Moon Street into a tizzy. When Benton realised it was from Carlton House, he delivered it to his young mistresses with a flourish. Anne and Melissa could not believe that it had not been issued by mistake. Mrs. Halcott was summoned immediately.

"Carlton House," Mrs. Halcott breathed, fingering the invitation almost reverently.

"Yes, but why would we be invited?" Anne asked. "Particularly now, when the new rumours are going about."

"Don't question your good fortune. It's the very thing. Do you realize that this invitation could put you back into good standing with the ton? No one will dare countenance the rumours if the Prince shows that he does not."

"But why?" Anne repeated perplexedly. "We are neither of the aristocracy, nor have we ever seen the Prince. Why should he condescend to take notice of us?"

"You must have a supporter among the haut ton who has access to the Prince's ear."

"Who?"

"Don't refine upon it too much, Anne. Just be thankful," Mrs. Halcott advised sagely. "Now, we must inspect your wardrobes to see if you have any clothes that will be suitable to wear there."

Anne dropped the subject as she and Melissa led Mrs. Halcott upstairs to inspect their gowns, but she continued to turn the puzzle over in her head. The only person she knew who had access to the Prince's ear was Lord Stanton. But why should he help her? The rumours might have ensured his winning the bet. Yet he had helped her before by having them invited to his sister's. Or was he hoping she would put a foot wrong before the exalted company at Carlton House? Or was Lord Stanton not involved at all? She gave up guessing. Perhaps Mrs. Halcott was right, and she should not refine upon it too much. She turned her full attention to Mrs. Halcott, who was discussing with Sanders the merits of two of Melissa's gowns. They were able to find gowns for both that would suit, which was a relief to Anne. She did not want to dig deeper into her rapidly dwindling funds.

Later that morning, Viscount Woolbridge came to call upon Melissa and asked her if she wished to ride with him in the Park that afternoon. Melissa accepted happily, and then, unable to keep their good fortune to themselves, showed the viscount their invitation.

"Carlton House? That is of all things wonderful!" he exclaimed, and then lest his enthusiasm seem to indicate that he was thinking of their besmirched reputations, he added, "I mean to say, I am invited that evening also, and would be happy to serve as your escort, Miss Amberly."

"Thank you, Lord Woolbridge," Melissa said. "I should be grateful for your escort."

As Anne watched the two converse, she felt it would not be long before the viscount approached her for permission to pay his addresses to Melissa. The gossip had not kept him away, and the devotion to Melissa, so plain in his hazel eyes, had never wavered. Melissa, looking demure in her simple rose sarcenet morning dress, was harder to read. She had not confided her feelings about her beaux to Anne. For the first time, this struck Anne as rather odd. She did not have long to reflect upon it, for Lord Millbank and his sister arrived. Melissa immediately made them acquainted with their good fortune in being invited to Carlton House.

"Pleased to be your escort, Miss Southwell," Lord Millbank said when it became apparent she had none, waving his scented handkerchief gracefully. He leaned against the mantelpiece, looking quite happy with the tippy figure he presented in his canary coat, striped waistcoat and cerulean blue neckcloth.

For a moment Anne's heart sank. She didn't want to go to Carlton House in the company of this young Tulip of Fashion. What if Lord Stanton were to see her with him? Then she was heartily ashamed of her reaction. Lord Millbank and his sister had been two of their staunchest supporters and best friends since they had arrived in London.

She accepted graciously and they made plans to go together in the viscount's large town carriage. The two gentlemen then departed, leaving Amelia, who wished to discuss the plans for her coming-out ball to be held the next week. Anne left Lady Amelia and Melissa happily deciding what they were going to wear, and took Sanders with her to walk to Hookam's for a new volume of poetry.

THE EVENING OF THE SUPPER at Carlton House, Sanders began dressing them a good four hours before they were due to leave. Her efforts were successful, for neither of them had ever appeared to such advantage. Melissa wore a gown of white silk richly embroidered in blue around the train. It clung to her slender figure gracefully, giving her an almost fairy-like appearance. Her sapphire necklace complimented the blue of the embroidery, and she wore blue-dyed ostrich feathers in her ebony hair. Anne wore a tunic of gold over a petticoat of white satin trimmed with a Spanish net of gold. The tunic was fastened in the front with a diamond brooch Mrs. Halcott had insisted on lending her, and a headdress of five ostrich feathers rested on her golden hair.

They knew their toilettes were successful by the look of admiration in their escorts' eyes. Lord Woolbridge bowed quite low over Melissa's hand, and Lord Millbank, after looking Anne over with one of his quizzing glasses, let it down, declaring himself quite satisfied with her appearance.

The men were quite magnificently apparelled themselves. Lord Woolbridge wore a blue velvet dress coat embroidered in silver, plain breeches of silk, a white satin waistcoat and the buckled shoes that were de rigueur for court dress. His chestnut hair was neatly dressed, but unpowdered. He could not compare with the magnificence of Lord Millbank, who had quite outdone himself. He was clad in a green velvet coat embroidered in gold, a white waistcoat elaborately embroidered in a rainbow of colours, velvet breeches edged in gold lace, white silk clocked stockings, and a heavily powdered wig. Anne felt quite underdressed beside him.

She was somewhat nervous as they approached Carlton House. Her life had not prepared her for entrance into such rarified society. Her first view of the brightly lit residence through the screen of Ionic columns on Pall Mall was almost intimidating. There was a huge crush of carriages, and it seemed an eternity before Lord Woolbridge's carriage was able to pull up before the classic porch.

As they worked their way through the crowds of people up the carpeted stairs and into the great octagon-shaped hall, Anne began to lose some of her nervousness in her anonymity. It was so crowded it was impossible for people to notice many of the others attending. She was also surprised to find that Lord Millbank's elaborate toilette was not at all out of the way in Carlton House. Most of those present were in court dress.

Lord Woolbridge and Lord Millbank proved to be excellent guides, and showed them through some of the open rooms of the Prince's residence. The interior was tastefully decorated, and Prinny's art collection was justly famous. They were admiring a particularly beautiful painting by a Flemish artist when a sudden hush of conversation indicated the Prince's arrival.

Anne and Melissa had never seen Prince George, and craned their necks trying to get a glimpse of him without appearing too obvious. The Prince and his entourage moved slowly through the crowd, the Prince stopping frequently to greet friends. Anne saw Beau Brummel among those with him, but did not recognize the others. As the Prince approached their vicinity, one of his entourage spoke into his ear, and the Prince looked at their group. Then to the astonishment of Anne and Melissa, he walked directly up to them.

"Present me to your beautiful companions, Millbank," he commanded, as the two women sank into deep curtsies before him.

The Prince first greeted Melissa, complimenting her on her beauty, and then turned to Anne. Anne found herself looking into a pair of bright and admiring blue eyes. She had heard the Prince was becoming quite corpulent, and was surprised to find him still a very handsome man. His well-cut coat hugged his shoulders, and if his brightly embroidered waistcoat strained about the middle, his breeches outlined a pair of still-shapely legs.

"Miss Southwell, your father would have been proud indeed to see what a beautiful woman you have become. Although Miss Amberly is enchanting, it will be a few years before her beauty reaches the maturity and perfection of yours."

He took her hand and pressed it warmly. Anne's heart quickened, and as she continued to look into his admiring eyes, she found that she was not immune to the legendary charm of Prince George. No wonder Mrs. Fitzherbert would tolerate so much and still love him.

The Prince released her hand and moved on, leaving Anne and Melissa in a daze. The Prince's attention to them had been very marked, and they felt quite overwhelmed. Several people who had noticed the Prince's interest in them came forward and asked to be presented. They found themselves the centre of a flurry of attention until the guests began to move up the great double staircase to the room where the dinner would be served.

The experience of Lord Millbank and Lord Woolbridge was invaluable in finding their places. Anne wondered how it had been arranged for Melissa's and her cards to be placed next to their escorts, and then dismissed it. No doubt one of the two had so notified the Prince's secretary. Servants began to place the dishes of the first course upon the tables, and they became so heavily laden with food that Anne thought they must surely collapse. The Prince was at his most democratic, and did not sit apart, but joined the guests at a table not far from theirs.

The dinner had nine courses and lasted for several hours. Anne and Melissa were only able to sample a few of what appeared to be hundreds of dishes placed on the tables through the dinner, but what they did taste was delicious. The talk of Prinny's good chefs was not exaggerated. Anne ate a dish of eels in truffle sauce with a feeling of bliss, and Melissa helped herself to more chicken quenelles several times. After two hours they were quite full, and unable to sample any of even the most tempting dishes, but the dinner continued for several hours more.

Finally the Prince had eaten his fill and rose from his table. This signalled a general exodus, and they once again fought the crush of people to leave the palace. Their driver was eventually able to manoeuvre their carriage up to the portico, and the four got into it with relief.

"Wasn't it wonderful?" enthused Melissa as they drove slowly down Pall Mall. "Imagine, the Prince of Wales picked you out of all the beautiful women present to notice, Anne."

Anne could not believe it was that simple, but she kept her suspicions about Lord Stanton to herself.

"You'll be overwhelmed by invitations now, don't you know," Lord Millbank said with satisfaction. "I say, Miss Southwell, few doors will be closed to you."

Anne smiled and reflected on the capriciousness of Society as the others discussed the evening. False words could cause their fall from grace, a smile and compliment from a dissolute if charming Prince could reinstate them. It was quite confusing. She had enjoyed the Season so far despite their problems, but she would be glad when Lord Woolbridge made an offer for Melissa and she could return to the more uncomplicated life in Medford.

AFTER THE SINGULAR ATTENTION paid to them by the Prince at Carlton House, Anne and Melissa found that they were indeed catapulted back into favour as quickly as they had been out. Invitations once again poured in, although the doors of Almack's remained closed, as did those of the highest sticklers of the ton. The Halcotts and their other friends were pleased with their return to favour. Anne continued to accept Captain Leslie's escort and her respect and affection for him continued to grow, but she was still unsure what to do once she won the bet and was free to entertain thoughts of marriage. A pair of dark eyes kept intruding on her thoughts of Captain Leslie's blue ones. Lord Stanton did not call again at Half Moon Street, but she saw him at Drury Lane, again in the company of Lady Parnell, and he always sought her hand for a dance at balls.

Anne took advantage of one such dance after the dinner at Carlton House to thank him for what she was sure was his part in re-establishing their credit.

"Why should you think I had anything to do with it?" asked Lord Stanton, amused at Anne's perception. "The Prince disliked seeing the daughters of loyal officers who died in his service treated so unfairly."

"Perhaps. But who brought the situation to his attention?"

"Now why should I do that when it would be to my disadvantage?"

"Your sense of fair play?"

"Very well, Miss Southwell, if you wish to think so," he replied as he escorted Anne from the dance floor.

"Do you think your credit is good enough to be seen speaking to me a moment," he asked, taking advantage of their temporary isolation.

"Yes," Anne replied, seating herself on a chair next to the wall.

"Green becomes you," Lord Stanton said, looking admiringly at the picture she presented in her green silk gown, a half handkerchief trimmed with flowers over her beautiful hair.

Anne found herself very aware of his presence, and a remembrance of a January evening at Longworth brought a blush to her cheeks.

"Now what caused that blush, I wonder," he teased. "You must govern your countenance more carefully or we shall be noticed."

"Of what did you wish to speak to me?" Anne asked, trying to will the blush away.

Lord Stanton's expression and attitude changed subtly, the smile leaving his dark eyes.

"I only wished to tell you that I have not despaired of winning our wager yet, so do not become overly confident. I am referring to Captain Leslie."

At the mention of Captain Leslie, Anne's good humour disappeared. "My friendship with Captain Leslie is my concern. In any case, I don't see how I can lose now. Melissa has several suitors."

"Do not forget that the marriage must take place before July and that the groom must be a member of the nobility," he said, looking meaningfully at the dance floor, where Melissa was partnered with Lieutenant Halcott.

Anne schooled her countenance to reveal nothing, but inside she seethed. Lord Stanton had as good as told her not to entertain thoughts of marriage since she was bound to become his mistress. The utter gall! She looked at the dancers and saw Melissa laugh at something Lieutenant Halcott said. Melissa looked very happy and carefree. *Could* she lose, she wondered. Was there more between them than she had been aware of?

"Ah! You see I may be correct, Miss Southwell," Lord Stanton said as he watched the thoughts flit across her face. "Don't delude yourself that I shall let you off the hook should your cousin choose to make a match with an untitled gentleman."

Anne made no response, and Lord Stanton rose with a sardonic smile. He bowed and left her.

Anne remained frozen on her chair, staring into the couples on the dance floor unseeingly. Her thoughts towards Lord Stanton had softened over the past weeks. She had come to think, somehow, that despite the two thousand pounds and his reminders of the wager, he would not really hold her to it. Particularly after his aid in re-establishing them in Society. His words showed that her conclusion had been incorrect. He *was* the rake Hell-born Harry. The charm was part of that, she realized. How could he be a successful rake if he didn't have charm? The dance ended, and Anne awoke from her daze as the couples left the floor and walked around her. Captain Leslie approached and took the chair Lord Stanton had vacated.

"What was Lord Stanton saying to distress you? I noticed your agitation from the dance floor."

"Nothing, Captain Leslie." Anne smiled with an effort. "It is only that the room is a little close and I have developed a headache."

Captain Leslie was immediately all concern and offered to notify her cousin and Mrs. Halcott of her indisposition. They made their excuses to their hostess and left soon after. Anne found that her imaginary headache had become all too real as she worried about her wager, and she went immediately to bed. A soft knock sounded at her door.

"Come in," Anne called, sitting up in bed.

Melissa entered and sat on the edge of the four poster.

"How are you feeling now? I asked Sandy to make a tisane, and she'll bring it up shortly. It will help you sleep."

"It is only a headache," Anne protested. "I will be fine in a little while."

Melissa looked doubtful and stroked Anne's forehead, her face showing concern. Anne closed her eyes, not wishing to look at Melissa's sweet face. If what Lord Stanton had hinted at were true, could she stand in her ward's way? She could, of course, simply refuse permission for Melissa to marry Lieutenant Halcott. She was Melissa's guardian and, until she came of age, Melissa could not marry without her permission. But that would do her no good, anyway, since part of the wager was that Melissa must marry by July. Anne could not force her to marry. And could she be that heartless, anyway? No. The wager was none of Melissa's doing. It was hers, and she must be the one to suffer its consequences. A line from a poem in a book she had borrowed from the circulating library recently came to mind—"The best laid schemes o'mice an' men gang aft a-gley."

Sanders entered with the tisane, and she and Melissa stayed to be sure she drank it all, Sanders with dire warnings about the effects of too much merrymaking at her age. After they left, Anne fell into a deep but troubled sleep.

Anne felt better the next morning. She dressed in a simple print frock and ate a good breakfast, then joined Melissa in the drawing room. Lieutenant Halcott paid a short morning call, and Anne observed his manner with Melissa closely. He and Melissa did seem very comfortable in each other's company, but she could detect none of the adoration in Lieutenant Halcott's eyes that was so obvious in Viscount Woolbridge's when he observed Melissa. Melissa became aware of Anne's close scrutiny, and looked at her questioningly. After Lieutenant Halcott had taken his leave, she came and sat next to Anne on the sofa.

"May I speak to you about something?" she asked.

"Of course."

"It is just that—well, what do you think of Lieutenant Halcott?"

Anne's heart sank at her cousin's words. Lord Stanton was right. He was more observant than she. She forced herself to overcome the panic she felt and answer truthfully.

"He is a fine gentleman and officer."

Melissa twisted her hands in her lap and looked at the floor. "It's just that I know you have your heart set on my marrying a title. You have done so much for me, I hate to disappoint you. But you see, I love Lieutenant Halcott."

"Has he spoken to you of marriage?"

"No, of course not. He would approach you first in the correct form. But I can tell..." she trailed off.

Melissa was looking at her anxiously, and Anne forced herself to smile.

"Yes, I did have hopes you would marry a title," she admitted. "But your happiness is most important. If you love Lieutenant Halcott and he returns your love, that is what matters. But I would ask you to make no firm decisions until the end of the Season. Things can change, and you may find that your feelings for Lieutenant Halcott are not as strong as you think."

"Oh, thank you," Melissa cried out. "I'll wait until the end of the Season, I promise. But I won't change my mind," she added.

Melissa looked at the mahogany clock on the mantelpiece.

"I promised to go walking with Lady Amelia," she said, "and if I don't hurry I shan't be there in time." She rose, and then bent down to drop a kiss upon Anne's cheek. "Thank you, best of guardians."

In a short time Anne heard Melissa and Sanders leave. Her thoughts in a turmoil, she rang and asked Benton for some ratafia, and instructed him she was not to be disturbed. She needed time to think things out. She began to pace the room as she had done that day in February. She had succeeded, and yet she had failed. It had never occurred to her that Melissa would choose to marry someone without a title. Melissa was so beautiful, her nature so sweet, that it had just seemed *right* that she marry a title and be pampered and spoiled the rest of her life. If she married Lieutenant Halcott her life would be very different.

She stood by the window, looking down into the street at the vehicles passing by. Well, her life mattered little, anyway. She should look on the bright side. She supposed she would be given a larger house by Lord Stanton and perhaps some jewels to add to her modest collection. She would refuse to appear with him in public as Lady Parnell did, though. Perhaps she could suffer through it with the fewest people becoming aware of it as possible.

She traced her finger idly over the back of the chair by the window. She might as well face it. She had lost the wager. There was no hope. She was bound to become Lord Stanton's mistress, however repugnant it might be to her. Anger at Lord Stanton overcame her, and she clenched her fists, remembering his words the night before. She tried to remind herself again that she was as guilty as he for entering upon the wager, but the anger remained. She might as well concede right now and get it over with. That would be better than waiting until the end of the Season, watching Lord Stanton's knowing smiles.

CHAPTER NINE

ONCE ANNE HAD DETERMINED to concede the wager, she wished to get it over with as soon as possible. The next morning she carefully went through the invitations, seeking one to a function that Lord Stanton would be likely to attend.

Melissa came into the drawing room looking so bright and happy that Anne could not regret her decision. Lieutenant Halcott was taking her for a drive, and she was clad in a becoming yellow morning dress trimmed with a narrow flounce. A stamp-paper hat trimmed in shades of yellow sat on her ebony curls, and she carried a green parasol.

Anne bade her good-morning and resumed looking through the invitations.

"I am trying to decide which function we should attend tonight," she said.

"Tonight is Amelia's come-out ball. We must attend that, of course," Melissa reminded her, and crossed the room to watch for Lieutenant Halcott's arrival from a window.

"Yes, I had forgotten," Anne said, putting the invitations back on the salver and seating herself on her favourite chair.

Melissa looked at Anne thoughtfully. She appeared to be quite distracted. Perhaps it had meant more to Anne for her to marry a title than she would admit. But if it was a title she wanted, Anne could marry one herself.

"Have you ever thought of Lord Millbank as a serious suitor?"

Startled by the question, Anne looked at Melissa in surprise, and then laughed. "No. I cannot see myself spending the rest of my life helping my husband deciding how many quizzing glasses or what colour of neckcloth to wear. Although I do like him, despite his absurd posturings."

"I thought perhaps if you did not care to marry Captain Leslie, Lord Millbank would be a possibility," Melissa persisted. "He *is* titled, and Amelia tells me he has never before paid the attention to any woman that he does to you."

"No, Melissa, I am not so determined on a title. Of the two I would prefer Captain Leslie if I were to marry, which I am not sure I shall."

"But every woman must wish to make a good match," Melissa said. "You did not have the opportunity in Medford, but here in London you could have many suitors."

Anne thought she had better lay the groundwork for her not marrying. It would not be possible for her ever to marry after she paid off her wager to Lord Stanton.

"It is true that when I was younger I thought of marriage," Anne explained. "But now after all my years of seclusion in Medford, I no longer find the idea attractive. I became quite used to the quiet life in the country and I miss it."

Melissa felt a little guilty. Here she had been enjoying the time in Town, while Anne was pining for the country. She had an idea.

"Why don't we arrange a picnic in the country," she suggested. "I know Amelia would enjoy it, and the Spencers might like to go as well."

Glad to have the subject changed, Anne agreed, and they began making plans. When Lieutenant Halcott arrived to take Melissa for a drive, he was apprised of the idea and entered into the planning. After they left, Anne felt that she had narrowly escaped Melissa's probings. If she were not careful, Melissa would suspect something was wrong. She must concede the wager and get it over with so she would not be so nervous. She would insist to Lord Stanton that she not pay it off until Melissa was safely married to Lieutenant Halcott, and out of danger of being affected by anything Anne might do. She hoped he would be at Lady Amelia's come-out ball tonight so she could do what must be done.

AS THEY ENTERED the Millbanks' house that night, Anne and Melissa were pleased to see that Lady Amelia was in exceptional looks. The excitement of the evening had brought a becoming flush to her cheeks, and she greeted Anne and Melissa with animation. She was clad in a flattering gown of white muslin, a garland of white flowers in her soft brown hair and a simple carnelian necklace at her throat.

Even Lady Millbank appeared less of a dragon, welcoming Mrs. Halcott and her protégeés with more warmth than usual. Other times she had been markedly cold to them, particularly to Anne. Perhaps, Anne suddenly realized, she feared Anne was trying to snare her son. The thought amused her, and she greeted Lord Millbank with a bright smile. Lord Millbank was dressed in honour of the occasion, dazzling in a lavender coat, green waistcoat, yellow breeches and no fewer than four quizzing glasses. He returned her smile and looked immensely satisfied with himself.

When they went into the ballroom, Anne looked around to see if Lord Stanton was present, but could not find him, although she did see Lord and Lady Brookfield. She also saw Lady Conliffe, in a gown of clinging white sarcenet, looking smug with Lord Woolbridge beside her. Perhaps Lord Stanton would come later, Anne decided, and tried not to worry too much. But as the evening progressed without Lord Stanton putting in an appearance, Anne began to be nervous. Perhaps he was not going to come at all. She became quite unable to concentrate, and even made mistakes in the dance steps while dancing the gavotte with Mr. Spencer. She sat the next dance out with Lord Millbank, who became rather puzzled when Anne assured him that he looked very fine in his new coat by Hoby and boots by Weston. Perhaps she did not feel quite the thing, he decided charitably, looking her over with one of his quizzing glasses. He fanned her a moment with his large canary-coloured fan, and then went to fetch her a glass of lemonade. Anne accepted it gratefully, and assured him she would be quite all right; she just needed to sit out a few dances. Lord Millbank offered to sit with her, but she refused graciously, saying she could not allow him to desert his other guests.

Sitting alone by the wall, Anne at last saw Lord Stanton arrive. She waited impatiently for him to come and claim his customary dance with her, and thought absently how much more flattering his conservative well-cut clothes were than Lord Millbank's extreme fashions. The close-fitting coat and breeches outlined his muscular form, and his neckcloth was tied in a perfection that rivalled Brummel's. But while she appreciated his looks, the sight of his confident figure also increased the animosity she was feeling for him since his warning that she not encourage Captain Leslie.

As soon as Lord Stanton caught sight of Anne by the wall, he came over to her and bowed.

"May I have the pleasure of the next dance, Miss Southwell?"

"Thank you, Lord Stanton, but it is quite close in this room, and I feel faint. Would you escort me for a turn upon the balcony?" she asked him abruptly.

"Do you know what you are saying, Miss Southwell? Are you sure you wish to go out on the balcony alone with me?"

"I do not think anyone will remark upon it, and if they do I am willing to take the risk to my reputation," she replied.

"Very well," Lord Stanton said, and giving her his arm, he escorted her through the balcony door. In their absorption with each other, neither noticed a young girl with black curls standing next to a potted plant to the left of the balcony door where she had gone to get a breath of fresh air.

"What is it you wish to discuss?" asked Lord Stanton as he guided her to the right corner of the balcony. "I hardly think you wished to come out here just to be in my company."

"No. I wish to concede the wager," Anne said coldly, her palms damp with nervousness.

"You wish to concede? The Season is barely half over," Lord Stanton said in astonishment.

"It makes no difference. You were correct in your appraisal of the situation," Anne informed him almost angrily. "Melissa indicated her partiality for Lieutenant Halcott to me yesterday. I will not stand in the way of her chance for happiness and force her to marry someone she doesn't love just for the sake of a title and to win my wager."

Lord Stanton hesitated. He found himself oddly reluctant to take what had been just offered. He leaned against the wrought-iron railing of the balcony and regarded Anne closely. She gazed back at him unwaveringly, her quickened breath causing her breasts to rise and fall under the russet silk of her gown, and her anger bringing a high colour to her cheeks.

"I must insist the wager stand," he said finally. "Much can happen before the Season ends. Has Halcott actually made an offer? If not, Melissa may yet marry a title. Or," he added, deliberately provocative, "are you that anxious to become my mistress?"

He stepped forward, placed his hands upon her shoulders and, catching her by surprise, bent down to kiss her. For a moment, Anne did nothing. Then anger took over, anger at Lord Stanton for ever tempting her to make the wager, anger at herself for accepting it, anger at his possessiveness. She broke free and tried to slap him, but he caught her wrist easily and held it. Then, to her mortification, he began to laugh.

"What has you in such a passion, my dear? Are you angry at me for being correct about your ward's affection for Lieutenant Halcott, or are you angry because you are losing? Didn't your brother ever tell you it is bad form to show emotion when you lose?"

So outraged that she could not trust herself to speak, Anne broke free and rushed back into the ballroom. In her agitation she failed to notice the flash of blue skirt as the girl standing to the left of the door pulled back farther behind the potted plant.

Shocked, Melissa waited quietly behind the plant until Lord Stanton, appearing unruffled by the encounter, went back into the ballroom, and then she followed unobtrusively through the door.

Across the room, another dark-haired girl had noticed Anne's dash into the ballroom, and watched with interest as Lord Stanton and Melissa followed her discreetly into the room.

Anne went to the retiring room, where she tried to gain time to get control of herself by pretending to inspect her hem for a tear, and then straightening her headdress. As she pretended to have a great deal of difficulty adjusting a feather to her liking, the door opened and Lady Conliffe came in.

"That is a most attractive gown, Miss Southwell," she said. "I look forward to the day I will be able to wear such colours," she added, smoothing her pink sarcenet.

"Thank you, Lady Conliffe," Anne replied. "I do not think the day is far off," she said, too angry to modify her response. Lady Conliffe appeared unoffended.

"Lady Amelia's ball is a great success, but it is also a sad crush, is it not?" she asked Anne. "One becomes quite overcome with the heat and needs a breath of fresh air."

Anne looked at her sharply, but Lady Conliffe's face betrayed nothing. "Yes, I believe I find I have a need of a breath of fresh air right now. Excuse me, please," she said to Lady Conliffe, walking to the door.

"As you say, Miss Southwell." Lady Conliffe smiled, rising to leave also. "I suggest the balcony."

As Lady Conliffe returned to the dance floor, Anne looked after her thoughtfully, wondering just what she had seen. Well, there was nothing she could do. She shrugged and prepared to endure the rest of the evening as best she could. She could not ask Melissa to leave her friend's come-out ball early. Fortunately, Lord Stanton appeared to have left, and because she no longer worried about encountering him, the time went by fairly quickly.

On the ride home that night, Anne forgot her own troubles due to Melissa's strange silence. Usually Melissa liked to discuss the entertainment they had attended, but tonight she sat in an odd, almost morose, silence. Mrs. Halcott noticed it, too, and questioned her, but Melissa simply said she was fatigued.

After Mrs. Halcott's driver stopped and left them at their town house, and Sanders disappeared with their pelisses, Melissa spoke abruptly.

"I wish to speak with you, Anne."

"What is it?" Anne inquired, uneasy at Melissa's tone.

"Perhaps it would be easiest if I told you that I overheard your conversation on the balcony with Lord Stanton. I assure you it was not intentional, but I was on the other side of the balcony where I had gone for a breath of fresh air."

Anne felt a cold hand grasp her heart. "Let us discuss this in my bedchamber," she said.

In strained silence they went upstairs and shut themselves in Anne's room. Melissa remained standing by the door, and Anne walked to the fireplace, where she stood for a moment, marshalling her thoughts.

"What exactly did you overhear?" she asked cautiously.

"Everything," Melissa said, looking directly at Anne. "What was the wager Lord Stanton mentioned? What did it have to do with my marrying a title?"

"It was nothing, Melissa," Anne replied, attempting to pass it off lightly. "Only a joke between us. You know how I like to wager."

"I know how you *used* to wager," Melissa replied. "Tell me the truth, Anne."

Anne felt uneasy in the presence of this new Melissa. Always before Melissa had been gentle and rather unassuming. This determination was a new aspect of her personality, one Anne was not sure she liked. As Melissa continued to regard her steadily, Anne knew that she must tell the unvarnished truth. Reluctantly, she sat on a chair by her bed and began her tale. Melissa remained standing, her hands clenching the silk of her skirts. When Anne finished her story, a silence remained unbroken between them for a long time.

"It was for me, wasn't it, Anne?" Melissa said at last, her tone flat and unemotional.

Anne knew that only the truth would be accepted. "I thought that if I could use the money I planned to use as your dowry for clothes and a better house, you would have a better chance to make a good match. The two thousand pounds made all the difference," she confessed.

"And you let me think well of Lord Stanton. He is indeed an unprincipled rake."

Anne found herself defending him. "He did not force me to enter upon the wager. I did that of my own accord."

"Perhaps. But he made the terms such that he knew you would not refuse," Melissa said perceptively. "Please forget our conversation of yesterday. I find I was mistaken in my heart. It is Viscount Woolbridge that I love."

"Melissa, don't do this," Anne pleaded. "There is no need. The wager is a joke. Lord Stanton has no intention of holding me to it."

Melissa looked at her almost pityingly. "I was on the balcony, Anne. I heard what was said."

"I will not give my permission for your to marry Lord Woolbridge," Anne said desperately.

"Then I will persuade him to elope to Gretna Green," Melissa said implacably. "I must retire now, Anne. This evening has been quite fatiguing."

Melissa left the room, closing the door behind her and leaving Anne alone with her guilt and misery. Anne feared this new Melissa would not waver in her determination. There must be an answer, some way out of this predicament, but at the moment she could think of none. She lay awake most of the night, hearing the sounds of the London night, but finding no answers in them.

SAFE IN HER ROOM, Melissa was unable to control the tears she had been fighting all evening. She dismissed Sanders and threw herself on the bed in a frenzy of weeping. All her hopes and dreams were dead. She could not marry Lieutenant Halcott. She would have to marry Viscount Woolbridge. And she could not even explain to Stephen. She did not blame Anne, for she had done what she had for her sake. It was the irony of it that it should be the cause of her losing the one thing she truly wanted. She cried and cried, not even stopping when Sanders, worried about her mistress, came into the room unbidden. Distressed by Melissa's uncontrollable grief, she tried to comfort her, but could not. Only when she said she was going to call Anne did Melissa speak, saying "No!" in such a harsh voice that Sanders could not believe it was her gentle Melissa speaking.

CHAPTER TEN

ANNE ROSE EARLY the next morning, despite her lack of sleep, hoping to speak with Melissa at breakfast. Melissa did not come down, though, but had a tray sent up to her room. Anne knocked on Melissa's door, but was told by a frosty Sanders that Melissa was preparing to go to Hookam's with Miss Spencer, and did not have time to speak with her.

Anne went to the drawing room, hoping Melissa would descend early, but not until Miss Spencer arrived did she make an appearance. Melissa's face showed no traces of the tears of the previous night, but her usually charming and unaffected manner was somewhat artificial and strained. Miss Spencer did not appear to notice, being full of the success of Lady Amelia's coming-out ball the night before.

After Melissa and Miss Spencer left, Anne rang for tea and sat in her favourite chair by the window, still trying to think of a way out of her difficulties. She had been there only a few minutes when Sanders came into the drawing room, her face stern.

"Miss Southwell, I would like to speak to you a moment."

Anne nodded, afraid she knew what Sanders wished to discuss.

"Something is troubling Melissa greatly," she said. "She spent most of last night crying. Do you know what it is?"

Anne's conscience smote her. She had turned out to be an unfit chaperone indeed. Because of her unguarded behaviour, Melissa, instead of happily making plans to marry the man she loved, was preparing to sacrifice herself for her guardian and marry another. It should be the other way around. She should be making sacrifices for Melissa.

"Yes, I know what is troubling Melissa, but there is nothing I can do about it at the moment. Don't worry, I will think of something soon."

Sanders looked at Anne sceptically, but realized that she had no intention of being more forthcoming. Well, she had done what she could by letting Miss Southwell know of Melissa's deep unhappiness. Although she couldn't totally approve of Miss Southwell, thinking her manners too free for a lady, she knew that she had a strong sense of duty and would do all she could for her ward.

After Sanders left the room, Anne sighed deeply and stared blindly out the window. She wished there were someone she could confide in and ask for advice, but there was no one. Anyone—except perhaps Lord Stanton, and he was the cause of her problems—would be shocked at the breach of etiquette that had gotten her into the situation. For a brief moment, she *did* consider asking Lord Stanton for advice, but when she remembered the scene on the balcony, her anger returned, and she knew she could not.

When Melissa returned from her walk, she found Anne still in the drawing room. Seeing the dark circles under her eyes, Melissa softened enough to speak.

"It is really not so bad, Anne. Lord Woolbridge is a fine man. He is well favoured, has a good nature and a title. One could not ask for more in a husband," she said. She saw that Anne was about to speak, and said, "I will discuss it no further. I am determined on my course. There is nothing you can do." She left the room before Anne could reply.

As the week went by and Melissa's resolve did not waver, Anne began to feel that there *was* nothing she could do. Melissa spent time most days with the viscount, and when the lieutenant called at his usual hour she was rarely home. Viscount Woolbridge, who had begun to think he was losing to his rival, now began to think he had a chance.

That Saturday was the day for which the picnic had been planned. With both Melissa and Lady Amelia planning, it had grown into quite a large outing, and when Saturday morning arrived, four carriages set out, not counting those carrying the servants and comestibles. Anne and Melissa rode in the carriage with Mrs. Halcott, escorted by Lieutenant Halcott and Captain Leslie on horseback.

Captain Leslie had suggested they go north of New Road, where there were open fields and farms with several little streams. It proved to be a delightful spot, and in spite of her worries, Anne began to enjoy herself. It was a beautiful day—the sun shone warmly, and wildflowers bloomed in profusion. As the servants unpacked the hampers, the guests strolled about in pairs or sat in the shade of the beeches, enjoying the quiet and the fresh air. Anne, knowing she was looking well in a walking dress of buttercup yellow muslin with long sleeves of white, a Venetian bonnet of twist and green walking boots, walked happily with Captain Leslie. But the captain unwittingly destroyed her good mood.

"I wonder if Miss Amberly knows how unhappy she is making Halcott," he said as they paused beneath a beech.

Anne followed his gaze to where Melissa, charming in a print muslin frock and straw bonnet trimmed with flowers, sat with Lord Woolbridge. Nearby, Lieutenant Halcott sat with Lady Amelia. He was paying polite attention to his partner, but every so often he would direct a bewildered look at Melissa and the viscount.

Anne sighed tiredly, and Captain Leslie looked at her with concern. "I'm sorry, I did not mean to sound critical of your cousin. It is just that I cannot help noticing a change in Miss Amberly's attitude towards Lieutenant Halcott this past week. Lieutenant Halcott is my friend, and I would help him if I could."

"I understand, Captain Leslie, but I would prefer not to discuss it," Anne responded almost rudely.

Captain Leslie politely changed the subject, but Anne's earlier enjoyment in the outing was gone. She had thought her imprudent wager endangered only herself, but she now saw how short-sighted she had been. It was making several people miserable. She even felt it in her heart to be sorry for Lady Conliffe. She must have thought she was going to regain her place in the viscount's affections until this past week.

The servants had finished setting out the food, and she and Captain Leslie walked slowly back to the others. The captain selected a comfortable spot on a rug beneath the shade of one of the beeches and went to fill a plate for Anne. While Anne waited for him to return, she unfurled her parasol and, holding it so the long green fringe shaded her eyes, observed Melissa while appearing to be viewing the rural scene.

Melissa and Lady Amelia sat alone, the viscount and Lieutenant Halcott having also gone to fill plates for their partners. Lady Amelia appeared to be absorbed in picking daisies and weaving a chain out of them. Melissa, unaware that she was being watched, had lost the bright fixed smile she had worn all morning, and a bleakness had appeared on her face, looking incongruous with her youthful complexion. Anne saw Melissa's chest heave with a sigh, and her eyes went to where Lieutenant Halcott stood waiting for the viscount to finish filling Melissa's plate before returning to Lady Amelia. Melissa's bleak expression changed to one of sorrow and longing, and she dropped her gaze to the ground. Listlessly she began to follow Lady Amelia's example and weave a daisy chain.

Guilt weighed more heavily than ever on Anne, and she looked away. Her sweet young cousin should not have had to face the unpleasant realities of life so soon, and it was her fault that she had. One of Melissa's sweet nature and delicate beauty was born to be protected from the harshness of the world. Anne had to admire the strength of character that had been hidden under the soft sweetness of Melissa's personality, but it should not have been brought out in the manner it had.

Her thoughts were interrupted by the return of Captain Leslie, who, aware of Anne's usually hearty appetite, had filled a plate with the choicest delicacies. Anne smiled and thanked him as she took the plate but looked at it with dismay. With misery and guilt constricting her throat and stomach, how was she going to be able to eat one bite, much less a whole plate of cold pigeon pie, boiled ham, bread, cheese, puffs and a tart?

"Miss Southwell, are you feeling quite the thing?" Captain Leslie asked with concern as he held a glass of lemonade out to her.

"I am quite well, Captain Leslie," Anne said with a smile, furling her parasol and laying it down beside her before taking the lemonade. "I am only trying to decide which to sample first."

She picked up a puff and forced herself to bite into it. She must not allow her feelings to spoil the day for the others. Captain Leslie seemed reassured and went to fill a plate for himself. When he returned, Anne had begun to make inroads on her plate, washing the food down with quantities of lemonade. She and Captain Leslie were joined by some of the other guests, and somehow Anne managed to laugh, talk and consume most of her food. But she was relieved when the others had eaten their fill and suggested they stroll down to the placid stream that meandered through the fields.

Anne's relief was short-lived, however, for they were soon joined by Lady Amelia and Lieutenant Halcott, and she was forced to observe Lieutenant Halcott's painful efforts to be attentive to Lady Amelia, although she could see his thoughts were elsewhere. Miss Spencer and her brother seemed to be the only ones behaving naturally, and Anne tried to enter into Miss Spencer's enthusiasm over the cowslips, the furze in full bloom and other country delights. She was grateful when the shadows began to lengthen and the company made its way back to the carriages, and congratulated herself on having gotten through a difficult day.

Anne's worst time of the day was yet to come, however. Melissa rode home with the viscount, leaving Anne to ride alone in the carriage with Mrs. Halcott. Mrs. Halcott took advantage of their solitude to question her about Melissa.

"My dear, if you know what has caused the coolness between my son and Melissa, please tell me so that I may make it right. It breaks my heart to see him so downtrodden."

She stopped for a moment, then continued.

"I never spoke to you of it before, Anne, but Colonel Halcott and I were very pleased at the way the wind was blowing. I know you had hopes of Melissa's marrying a title, and to be sure she could have, but although he hasn't a title, Stephen is of gentle blood and would make her a good husband," she said with pride.

Anne found herself in the position of having to prevaricate to her good friend and sponsor. She could only assure Mrs. Halcott that she promoted the match, too, and promise to do what she could to mend the rift. And as they rode home the rest of the way in silence, it came to her that perhaps there *was* one thing she could do if she had to.

LORD STANTON WAS AS MYSTIFIED as the rest of Society by the sudden unmistakable preference of Melissa for Lord Woolbridge. The betting at White's, which had strongly favoured the Incomparable Miss A. making a match with Lieutenant H. now shifted to favour Viscount W. Anne had been the only one who had not seen Miss Amberly's preference for the lieutenant. What was behind the change? Could Anne have told Melissa of the wager? She had been very angry that day. He quickly rejected the idea. No, she would not do anything so unkind. He determined to question Anne about the situation, and went to enlist the aid of his sister, who was holding a rout party that evening to which Anne and her ward had been invited.

As he handed his cane and top hat to Lady Brookfield's footman, his sister came into the hall on her way out, clad in a blue jaconet walking dress and fawn-coloured pelisse.

"Could I have a word with you before you leave, Caroline? It is important."

Lady Brookfield looked at her brother assessingly. "Yes, I was just on my way to the milliner's. Come with me," she said, dismissing her maid and leading the way into a small salon.

"What is it, Harry?" she asked, seating herself on a delicate Hepplewhite chair with a heart-shaped back.

"I need your help in talking privately to Miss Southwell at your rout tonight."

Lady Brookfield considered refusing unless her brother told her what he was up to, but decided it was not time to force his confidence.

"I'll help if you'll give your word you intend the girl no harm. I cannot have her reputation destroyed in my home. I quite like Miss Southwell, and her ward, too."

"I have no intentions of seducing her in your house, dear sister."

"Very well. If she attends I will take her apart from the company on some excuse, but I can give you no more than half an hour."

"That's all I need," he replied.

ANNE ALMOST DID NOT ATTEND the rout that evening. She had a feeling Lord Stanton would be there, and did not wish to answer questions about Melissa's sudden preference for the viscount. Then she realized that if he did not see her at the rout party he was perfectly capable of calling upon her at Half Moon Street. She would rather face him at his sister's. Melissa, however, did refuse to go, pleading a headache. Anne did not believe her, but chose not to challenge her decision and went alone with Mrs. Halcott.

Anne did not know whether to be glad or sorry that she did not see Lord Stanton when they arrived at the rout. She was speaking to Mrs. Halcott and Mrs. Spencer when she was surprised to be approached by her hostess, who asked her if she would be willing to examine a new pianoforte she had purchased, as she knew Miss Southwell was an accomplished musician. Flattered, Anne agreed, and followed Lady Brookfield from the room and upstairs. Lady Brookfield stopped outside a door and addressed her.

"I hope you will forgive my subterfuge, my dear. My brother requested that I arrange a way in which he might have a private conversation with you without its being remarked. I agreed to help him, but I also told him it would be up to you."

Anne just wanted to get the interview over with. "Yes, I will speak to him."

"He is here in the library, then. I will come for you in half an hour." Lady Brookfield opened the door, holding it for Anne to pass through, and closed it behind her.

Lord Stanton rose from his seat by the fire. "I knew you would come, Miss Southwell. Please sit down," he said, motioning to a striped sofa. "What is this about Melissa and Lord Woolbridge? You surely did not tell your ward of our wager?"

Anne sat on the sofa and told of Melissa's overhearing their conversation on the balcony and her subsequent determination to marry Lord Woolbridge.

As Anne told him what had happened, Lord Stanton drummed his fingers upon the mahogany table next to his chair, undecided as to what course he should take. The honourable thing would be to release Anne from the wager, but he was reluctant to do so. It was his only means for continuing contact with her.

Anne waited in silence, hoping he would offer to release her from the wager. She wished only to forget the whole mess her imprudent behaviour had gotten her into. She regarded him steadily, noting his tight-fitting cream-coloured breeches, dark green coat and snowy cravat. Several minutes passed without either speaking, and she realized he was not going to co-operate. She would have to suggest the one way out that she had been able to think of.

She spoke, her voice flat. "It has occurred to me that there is a way in which I could persuade Melissa to reinstate Lieutenant Halcott in her affections. If I were to pay off the wager now, Melissa would have nothing to gain by refusing to marry Lieutenant Halcott."

Lord Stanton looked at her in astonishment. "Do you know what you are saying, my dear?"

"Yes, my lord, I do." Their looks caught and held. Without a word, Lord Stanton got up, removed his coat and joined her on the sofa. He turned Anne's face to his and lightly caressed it. Anne did not pull away or flinch, but neither did she respond.

With a muffled curse, Lord Stanton swept her into his arms, holding her closely, and placed his lips upon hers. Anne lay unmoving in his embrace, still angry and determined not to give him the satisfaction of a response, but her traitorous body had a desire of its own. Lord Stanton must have felt the almost imperceptible softening of the lips beneath his, for his kiss became gentle, tantalising, and his hand caressed her back through the material of her dress.

Anne was unexpectedly overwhelmed with a sensation of deep tenderness for the man beside her. The intensity of the emotion frightened her until she realised with sudden clarity what it was—love. She loved Lord Stanton. With that realisation she forgot where she was and what she was doing, aware only of a great yearning for the man she was with. Her tense body relaxed involuntarily, causing Lord Stanton's lips and hands to still in surprise. Abruptly, his arms tightened around her, crushing her gown, and his kiss became hard and rough for a moment before he suddenly thrust her from him and stood up.

"No," he said hoarsely. "I consider the wager made void by your cousin's overhearing our conversation. There is no honour in winning in such a manner. You may tell your ward that, and if she refuses to accept it, tell her you have already paid. She would not allow such a sacrifice to go for nothing."

Without another glance at her, Lord Stanton picked up his coat and left the room.

Shakily Anne rearranged her clothing and sat up. What had happened? Had her behaviour given Lord Stanton reason to leave her in disgust? Now that she was willing to give him what he desired, did he, perversely, no longer want her? Misery that her love had led to his rejection almost made her dissolve into tears, when a light tap at the door called her to herself.

Hesitantly, Lady Brookfield entered. "Forgive me, my dear, but the half-hour is passed. I thought I would accompany you back to the party." She paused as she took in Anne's dishevelled state and red eyes.

"Are you feeling quite the thing, Miss Southwell?"

Anne regained her composure with an effort. "I am quite all right, Lady Brookfield."

"I see you have been overcome with the headache. Would you like me to notify Mrs. Halcott and call your carriage?"

"Thank you, my lady," Anne answered tremulously. "I should be most grateful."

This time it was Anne's turn to be silent during the ride home in the carriage. Mrs. Halcott put it down to her headache, although it did not explain her red eyes. When Anne arrived home, she went up to Melissa's bedchamber and requested to speak to her privately. Sanders looked at her curiously, but left without a word. Anne sat upon a chair and colourlessly informed Melissa that Lord Stanton had called off the wager. Melissa, her perceptions heightened by her own love for Lieutenant Halcott, sensed there was a great deal more to the situation than Anne was telling her but let it pass.

"If you truly feel you have been released from the wager, then I will not marry Viscount Woolbridge. It is fortunate that he had not yet approached you for permission to make an offer. Although," she added in an attempt to lighten the atmosphere, "I think Society is going to label me a heartless flirt."

Anne tried to smile, but it was a sad effort, and Melissa did not attempt to keep her when she said she wished to retire. She did send Sanders to her with a tisane.

Tonight the tisane was not as effective, for Anne lay awake a long time, unable to sleep, unable to cry. Her misery was too deep for tears. How could she have come to love Lord Stanton? He was a dissolute rake. She didn't know how she had come to love him, but she did know that life without him would be totally unbearable. But somehow she would have to face it, because he had made it very clear that he didn't want her. He had thrust her away and left her as though he found her distasteful. But why? She tossed in her bed. That was what she didn't understand. He was a rakehell, after all, and she had only been giving him what a rakehell presumably wanted. It must be that she had betrayed her feelings for him.

Yes! That must be it. As a rake, he would not want love from her, not the kind she felt, anyway. He had made it quite clear from the beginning what he wanted from her, and she had not played the game. Not only had she lost the man she loved, she had lost her pride. It was a nightmare.

If she could do what she wanted, she would return to Medford and bury herself for the rest of her life in the quiet village. It had eventually assuaged the pain from the deaths of her father and brother; surely it would also do that to the pain of loving someone who did not love her in return.

But there was Melissa. She could not take her out in the middle of the Season. Particularly not now that she must return the two thousand pounds. Melissa was her ward, her responsibility. She could not abdicate her role. Somehow she would have to put a good face on things and get through the remainder of the Season.

WHEN THE MARQUESS LEFT his sister's house, he went directly to Lady Parnell's. That lady, since her husband was still out of town, made Lord Stanton welcome. She relaxed on a roll-backed sofa in her bedchamber, her silk nightdress falling open invitingly.

"You have not come to see me recently," she reproached him, as he helped himself to a glass of sherry from a decanter on a table. "Have you forgotten your old friends?"

"How could I do that?" Lord Stanton drawled, looking at her meaningfully. She *was* beautiful, slender and with satin-smooth skin. He quickly downed his sherry, and sat beside her on the sofa, pulling the pins from her silver-blonde hair. As it fell to her shoulders, she raised her hand to his head, pulling it down to hers, and kissed him softly on the lips. But for some reason, tonight her beauty did not have the power to stir him. As Lady Parnell began to untie his neckcloth, he pulled away.

"Not tonight, my dear. I have just remembered a pressing engagement."

The expression on Lady Parnell's face changed from one of enticement to one of vexation. She knew the signs. There was someone else. Lord Stanton had tired of her. Her displeasure showed as he kissed her hand and left.

Lady Parnell remained on the sofa, a frown on her face. She knew what to expect—in a few days she would receive a beautiful piece of jewellery, a farewell gift. She felt some regret, then shrugged. There was always another ready to take his place.

LORD STANTON RETURNED to his town house where he went to his study and ordered a bottle of port. He poured himself a full glass and leaned back in his wingback chair, trying to make sense out of his contradictory feelings. Anne Southwell had thoroughly bewitched him. He had had the opportunity to have what he so ardently desired since first seeing her at Longworth, and he had not taken it. What was wrong with him?

Instead, that insane desire he had had to protect her the day he heard Sedgewick maligning her had returned. He would not, could not, encumber himself with a wife. He would avoid her until he was no longer so besotted. He sat in his study until he had finished the bottle of port and then staggered upstairs. Lewis helped him undress and put him into his bed, wondering what had upset him so. It was very unlike Lord Stanton to drink himself into a stupor.

EARLY THE NEXT MORNING he was awakened by his valet, who informed him that his sister had called and refused to leave until she spoke to him. He groaned. What a devil of a head he had. Grumpily, he told his valet to inform his sister he was indisposed. Lewis did not have a chance to do so, however, before the door to his bedchamber opened and his sister invaded his room uninvited.

"I will not leave until you speak to me, Henry," she declared, pulling a straight-backed chair up to the bed and seating herself upon it. "Now, what did you do to Miss Southwell last night? The poor girl looked as though you had tried to ravish her. Did you?"

Lord Stanton raised himself up on one elbow and looked at his sister balefully. How dared she look so fresh and alert. "I assure you, Miss Southwell was unharmed."

"Then what is going on?"

"None of your business," he growled, "but you may rest assured that I will be staying away from Miss Southwell in the future."

Lady Brookfield took in her brother's dishevelled appearance thoughtfully. He looked burnt to the socket, which was not like her brother. There was something going on here—and she thought she knew what it was, if he did not. She had never before seen her brother so upset over a woman. Perhaps her brother was finally going to get his comeuppance. His interest in Miss Southwell went beyond mere desire; of that she was sure.

"Well, say your piece and have done with it," her brother said impatiently.

To his surprise, his sister did not subject him to a dressing down, but suddenly smiled and stood up.

"Later," she said as she left the room. "Meanwhile I recommend a raw egg mixed with beer and milk. It always works for Brookfield."

CHAPTER ELEVEN

AFTER THE FATEFUL NIGHT of Lady Brookfield's rout, Anne found it easier than she had expected to put on a cheerful face. She felt like an actress playing a part. All she had to do was say the right lines and make the proper facial expressions.

Melissa did not seem to notice anything amiss. She was preoccupied with trying to reinstate Lieutenant Halcott and replace Viscount Woolbridge in her affections without doing it too obviously. She continued to be seen in the company of the viscount, but she gradually saw him less and the lieutenant more. Anne felt sorry for the viscount. He must see that the Incomparable Miss Amberly again preferred Lieutenant Halcott to himself, but must wonder what accounted for his fall from grace. Anne observed that he did not return his attentions to Lady Conliffe, though. Perhaps he had heard of her involvement in spreading the rumours, or perhaps he felt wooing Toasts of the Town had proved more trouble than it was worth.

Melissa was the first to notice that Viscount Woolbridge seemed to be becoming interested in Lady

Amelia. They had been much in each other's company most of the Season, since Amelia was Melissa's closest friend, but Lord Woolbridge had been so busy making sheep's eyes at Melissa that he had not noticed her friend. Now he suddenly seemed to take notice of her. Melissa commented on it to Anne, and the next time they were both at Half Moon Street, Anne watched them closely. It did appear to be true. Viscount Woolbridge no longer focussed all his attention on Melissa but sat next to Lady Amelia and seemed to be quite taken with her quiet charms. Anne had a feeling of satisfaction.

While this state of affairs pleased Anne, it had the opposite effect on Lady Conliffe. Her determination to destroy Miss Amberly and Miss Southwell in the eyes of Society gained renewed strength. The inquiries she had made in Bath and Brighton had proved fruitless, but the servant she sent to Medford came back with some very interesting information. She put on her gloves to make morning calls with anticipation. She would have her revenge at last.

ANNE DID NOT SEE LORD STANTON at any functions after the night at his sister's, for which she was grateful. She heard gossip of escapades he was getting into with the Carlton House set. Anne didn't care where he spent his time, as long as it was away from her. She felt that after her betrayal of her feelings and his rejection that she could conceal her anguish if she did not see him. All in all, she felt she was doing a good job of hiding her heartbreak.

One person, however, was not deceived by Anne's acting. The same morning Lady Conliffe's servant returned from Medford, Lieutenant Halcott and Captain Leslie arrived together at Half Moon Street. The lieutenant asked Melissa to accompany him on a walk, but to Anne's surprise, the captain did not invite her to go.

After the other two left, he stood looking out the window for a moment, running his fingers through his blonde hair. Eventually, he seated himself next to Anne on the sofa and gently took her hand. He looked at her affectionately, thinking how charming she appeared in her lavender round dress trimmed in purple, a matching cap upon her hair.

"Miss Southwell, I am going to presume upon our friendship again and ask what it is that is disturbing you lately. I can see your heart is not in things."

"Forgive me, Captain Leslie," Anne replied, smiling at him and answering lightly. "It is only a temporary indisposition. I hope I have not been casting a pall on everyone's pleasure."

"No, Miss Southwell, you dissimulate well. I only notice because of my affection for you. Please confide in me. You know that I only await your word to have the right to take all your problems upon myself."

Anne knew that she could not continue to let Captain Leslie hope after her realisation of her feelings for Lord Stanton. She had been remiss not to have informed him sooner. She drew her hand away and spoke.

"Captain Leslie, I shall never forget the honour you did me to make me an offer. But I must ask you not to renew your suit. I have come to know, only recently, that I cannot accept."

She looked at him steadily, hating herself for the pain she knew she must be causing him.

Captain Leslie smiled sadly at Anne. "I have known, somehow, that you had come to that decision. There is someone else, isn't there?"

"Yes, there is," Anne answered truthfully.

"Does he return your affections?"

"No. But it would not be fair to you to give you only half my heart."

"I would tell you it didn't matter, but I know you would never give yourself at all where you could not give yourself completely." He was silent a moment, then added, "I hope to remain your friend. If you should ever require assistance, call upon me."

"Thank you, Captain Leslie. I should have been sorry to lose your friendship and support."

Anne smiled at him again, tentatively, wishing she could give him what he desired. He lifted her hand again and placed a light kiss upon it.

"Good-bye, Anne," he said, standing.

Anne had the feeling the word held a different meaning this time that it had before. "Good-bye," she said, knowing that the next time she saw him it would be very different between them. The easy affection that had characterised their relationship would not longer be there.

She remained seated on the sofa after Captain Leslie had left, feeling quite cast down. She wished she had never left Medford. She seemed to be causing nothing but sorrow for those persons she cared most about. She sighed. At least Melissa was happy again. It would not be long before Lieutenant Halcott applied for her hand. She remembered that she had not yet returned the two thousand pounds and went to the desk to write out a bank draft. The thought of Lord Stanton plunged her into deeper misery. Why couldn't she have loved a good man like Captain Leslie? Why did she ever have to meet Lord Stanton? It would have been better if she had never known the kind of love she felt for Lord Stanton. Much better not to know what one was missing then to have a taste, only to have it snatched away.

She was still seated at her desk when Melissa returned from her walk with Lieutenant Halcott.

"It's the oddest thing, Anne," she said, drawing off her lilac gloves and taking a seat near Anne, "but Lady Fanning did not acknowledge my nod when we passed her near Hookam's. Then when we passed Miss

Spencer and Miss Armstrong in the street, they turned to look at a window, pretending they hadn't seen us."

"I'm sure you are imagining things, Melissa," Anne said reassuringly. "They probably truly didn't see you."

"Perhaps, but I have a strange feeling something is wrong. Maybe we shouldn't go to Lady Roberts's musicale tonight."

"Nonsense. We have been looking forward to it. Lady Roberts has promised some very talented musicians."

"If you are sure," said Melissa, thoughtfully taking off her gypsy hat and swinging it by the ribbands.

"I'm sure," said Anne getting up from the desk and ringing for Benton. She would have the bank draft delivered to Lord Stanton immediately. "You are overly sensitive because of our previous troubles," she reassured Melissa.

AS SOON AS THEY ENTERED Lady Roberts's town house that night, however, Anne knew that Melissa had been correct. There was something dreadfully wrong. Their hostess welcomed Mrs. Halcott with restraint, but said nothing whatsoever to Anne and Melissa. Conversations seemed to die as they walked through the room, and when they sat down for the performance, chairs near them emptied and remained so.

Melissa's face was white with mortification, and Anne felt her heart begin to beat rapidly with anger. What now! What social solecism could they possibly have committed? She could feel Mrs. Halcott tense beside her, but that lady gallantly behaved as though nothing were wrong. Anne and Melissa tried to emulate her, focussing their attention on the performance, and applauding when it was over, but they could not have said who performed or what they sang.

When the entertainment ended, Mrs. Halcott took Anne and Melissa with her as she went to speak to a few of her closest friends. These women did not let her down, and acknowledged her protégées, albeit reluctantly. The minutes seemed an eternity to Anne and Melissa, but Mrs. Halcott made them stay a full hour after the singing had ended. Then, when others began to leave, she allowed them to do so, as well.

In the carriage, Mrs. Halcott finally spoke, her bosom heaving indignantly. "I must get to the bottom of this immediately. I cannot understand what has happened that you should be cut so completely."

Anne and Melissa echoed her bewilderment. When the carriage stopped at their town house, Mrs. Halcott said, "I will find out what is behind this and return to tell you. Wait up for me please."

Anne and Melissa gave their pelisses to Sanders and went soberly up to the drawing room to wait for Mrs. Halcott's return. They searched their minds for some possible infringement of the rules, but could come up with none.

"Do you suppose it is the rumours of our finances or the one about you again?" asked Melissa.

Anne shook her head. "No, even at their height we were not cut as devastatingly as we were tonight. It must be something else, but I cannot imagine what."

It was two hours later when Mrs. Halcott returned, looking tired and defeated. Anne and Melissa waited anxiously for her to tell them what she had discovered.

"It is bad, very bad indeed," Mrs. Halcott said with a terribly serious expression. "I only hope that there is no truth in what I have been told, for if there is, there is no hope."

She shook her head gravely and took a deep breath.

"The *on dit* is that you and Melissa spent several days alone at Lord Stanton's estate. I must ask you—is there any truth to this?"

Anne looked at Melissa in dismay. They had not imagined anyone would ever hear of their stay at Longworth. Anne reached for Melissa's hand and pressed it reassuringly before answering Mrs. Halcott. She did not consider trying to evade the truth. She explained about the storm on their way to London and their two days at Longworth.

"But nothing improper occurred. I would have explained all this to you before, but I did not think it mattered. It was an accident that we stayed there, and Sanders and I were there to chaperone Melissa."

Mrs. Halcott sighed deeply.

"Thank you for being frank with me. I do not blame you for not telling me before. You could not foresee that problems might arise from it. It is to Lord Stanton's credit that he did what he could to protect your reputations. It is also true that you were there with Melissa. But you are an unmarried lady, Anne, whatever your age, and Sanders does not qualify as a proper chaperone, either. I'm afraid that with someone of Lord Stanton's reputation it simply isn't enough. I have no idea what to do. I know of no way to re-establish you in Society."

"But how did this get out, Mrs. Halcott?" Anne questioned. "No one knew but Lord Stanton and ourselves. I cannot believe that he would have let anything slip."

Melissa, whose opinion of Lord Stanton had deteriorated since the scene she saw on the balcony, was not so sure, but she remained silent.

"Someone made inquiries in Medford. I understand the story came from your coachman."

Lady Conliffe! It could only be she, thought Anne, and voiced her thought aloud.

"I have no doubt you are right, Anne, but knowing the source of the information does us no good. You *did* stay there unchaperoned, and even if nothing happened, no one would believe it. The damage is done. You do not have the wealth or social position to weather such a storm."

Mrs. Halcott looked sorrowfully at them, feeling at a loss.

"I am more sorry than I can say that this has happened. I feel that I have failed the memory of your father. Don't think that we will abandon you, but I fear we can do little to re-establish your credit. I must prepare you for the worst. You will no doubt be cut by most of your acquaintances wherever you go. And the gentlemen who do not cut you will be recognizing you for reasons best not gone into."

She sat in silence for a moment, then rose. "I must go now and confer with Colonel Halcott. Perhaps he will have an idea how to deal with the situation."

She leaned down to hug both of her protégées affectionately, promising that she, at least, would not desert them.

After she had gone, Melissa, who had remained silent while Mrs. Halcott was there, suddenly burst into tears, covering her face with her hands and rocking back and forth on the sofa.

"Oh, Anne. What will I do? Stephen—Lieutenant Halcott—will have nothing to do with me now."

Anne put her arms around Melissa and held her, trying her best to soothe her unhappy cousin.

"Melissa, my darling, if Lieutenant Halcott truly loves you it will make no difference to his feelings. You heard Mrs. Halcott say that they do not intend to abandon us."

But Melissa would not be comforted. Sobs continued to shake her body until she had no tears left. Anne sat with her until the early hours of the morning, when Melissa fell asleep from exhaustion. Anne stood up carefully so as not to wake Melissa, and went in search of Sanders. She explained the events of the evening to her, and the two went back to the drawing room, Sanders taking a blanket.

"I told you no good would come from staying at that rake's house," she said, covering Melissa with the blanket and preparing to sit up with her all night if necessary. Anne placed a light kiss on Melissa's tear-streaked cheek and went to bed, feeling she had failed in her duty to her ward.

THE NEXT MORNING Anne and Melissa went down to breakfast late, with dark circles showing under their eyes. They said very little to each other and were picking aimlessly at their food when Benton came in.

"Lieutenant Halcott is below, Miss Southwell, and asks to be allowed to speak to you."

Melissa gasped as the lieutenant strode into the room, not waiting for permission. He bowed and briefly bade them good-morning, then addressed Anne.

"Please forgive me for interrupting your meal, but I felt the urgency of the matter overcame social conventions. May I speak to you privately, Miss Southwell?"

"Of course, Lieutenant Halcott," Anne replied, rising from the table. While Melissa watched with apprehension apparent on her face, Anne led the lieutenant into the drawing room. She seated herself on the sofa, but Lieutenant Halcott remained standing. He came straight to the point of his visit.

"Miss Southwell, I have come to ask for Miss Amberly's hand in marriage. I had intended to wait until the Season was over, because I wished her to be very sure of her mind. She has the opportunity to marry into the aristocracy, and I wished her to be very sure she would prefer the life of an officer's wife. However, now I feel the circumstances warrant my applying earlier."

"Your affections *are* engaged, Lieutenant Halcott?" Anne queried. "This is not some quixotic gesture to save a young girl's honour?"

"No, Miss Southwell," he assured her. "My parents have known of my intentions for some time, and approve. They also concur that I should make my offer now. If it is seen that I offer for Melissa, many will realize that she is innocent of any improper behaviour. There will always be some who doubt, but enough will be convinced."

Anne looked at him searchingly and he gazed back at her, his brown eyes unflinching. His sincerity was apparent, and Anne felt a great load lift from her conscience. The lieutenant would make a good husband for Melissa. He was young but steady and reliable, and it was evident he did care deeply for Melissa.

"Then it only remains for me to tell you that Melissa's dowry is two thousand pounds, and that I give you permission to speak to her. I am sure she is waiting anxiously. Please rejoin her in the morning room."

Lieutenant Halcott thanked her warmly and went immediately to the morning room without waiting for Benton to escort him.

Anne remained in the drawing room, feeling much heartened. Melissa would not suffer for things that were none of her doing. The only difficulty would be for her to come up with two thousand pounds from her own funds, since she had had to return the two thousand to Lord Stanton. She could do it if she went back to Medford soon and lived very quietly. She was contemplating a return to the quiet village life when Benton announced another visitor.

"Lord Millbank."

Lord Millbank entered, splendidly apparelled in a pea-green coat with a wasp waist, yellow pantaloons, a striped waistcoat and a neckcloth that was a marvel of starch and intricate knots.

Anne appreciated the show of support he was making by calling upon her after her disgrace and welcomed him warmly. To her surprise, he seemed to have lost his studied attitude of ennui, and appeared nervous, toying with the chains hanging from his waistcoat, and even disarranging his immaculate neckcloth, pulling at it in a distracted manner. Suddenly, to her surprise, he lowered himself to his knees and caught her hand.

"Miss Southwell. You must be aware of the high regard in which I hold you. I would be pleased if you would do me the honour of accepting my hand in marriage," he said, placing a kiss upon her hand.

Anne was caught completely off guard by the proposal, and looked at Lord Millbank in astonishment. She was also deeply touched, for she knew that her disgrace in the eyes of Society would be hard for Lord Millbank to bear. She withdrew her hand from his slowly and begged him to rise.

"Lord Millbank, I am deeply honoured, more than I could ever express, but I cannot accept."

She thought she caught a glimmer of relief in his eyes as he rose from his position on the floor, but he still protested.

"Please consider it seriously, Miss Southwell. You need someone to protect your name. Think we'd suit admirably. You have an eye for colour that is rare in a female."

Anne smiled in spite of herself. "Thank you, Lord Millbank, but I must tell you that my heart is already engaged. If it were not for that I should be most pleased to accept your flattering offer."

Lord Millbank accepted her refusal gracefully. "Hope we will remain friends," he said. "M'sister and I will call later."

He lifted Anne's hand to his lips, bowed over it elegantly and took his leave. Anne noted with amusement that he strutted more than ever when he left, evidently proud of his chivalrous attempt to save her good name.

As soon as Lord Millbank departed, Melissa came into the drawing room, her whole being glowing, greatly transformed from the miserable girl of that morning.

"Anne, I'm so happy. You were right, Stephen did not believe the rumours. He says they will die down soon and won't affect us, anyway, as his regiment will be going to Brighton. What was Lord Millbank doing here so early?" she added.

Anne smiled at her. "It seems this is a morning for proposals. He made me an offer."

"Did you accept?" asked Melissa, looking surprised.

"No. Although I thought more of him than I ever have. He has a depth I did not suspect."

Melissa agreed it had been a chivalrous gesture, wishing for a moment that Anne had accepted, for that would have made her best friend a close connexion, and then her attention returned to her own happiness.

"We would like to be married the first of next month, before Stephen's regiment leaves. Could it be managed? Stephen says his mother will help."

Anne assured her they would manage, and Melissa left the room on a cloud, anxious to tell her Sandy of her happiness.

Anne went to her desk to begin planning. If the wedding was going to be so soon she would have to get busy. She was working on a list of things to be done when Benton came to the door, a fierce glare on his young face. He had not yet mastered the impassivity of a butler's expression that was required.

"Lord Stanton," he said, looking as though he would rather remove the caller forcibly from the premises. The servants knew of their mistress's fall from grace, and had no good feelings towards the cause of it.

Anne rose from her chair in shock. What was Lord Stanton doing here? She could not control the leap of her heart as she saw him, but it quickly subsided as she saw the bleak look in his eyes. He was impeccably clad as always, in a blue coat, buff pantaloons and waistcoat, white cravat, and black hair *à la* Titus, but his sartorial perfection was somehow off-putting. He greeted her stiffly and stood in the middle of the room, facing her.

"Miss Southwell, I came to assure you I had nothing to do with the story of your stay at Longworth becoming known, and to make what reparation I can by offering you the protection of my name. Will you do me the honour of becoming my wife?''

Anne remained frozen, standing before her chair. Here, then, was the offer she had dreamed of receiving in the secret corners of her heart. Yet it was nothing like she had imagined. This Lord Stanton was a stranger, stiff and formal. It was obvious he made the offer not from any regard for her but from the same notion of chivalry that had inspired Lord Millbank. Only Lord Millbank's offer had been much more gracious, she thought angrily.

''Thank you, my lord, for your generosity, but there is no need,'' she said coldly. ''Lieutenant Halcott has made an offer for Melissa this morning, so you see her reputation is safe, and for mine I care nothing.''

''I see,'' said Lord Stanton, his voice becoming more austere. ''But although you don't care at this moment you may in the future. It will be unlikely that anyone will ever offer for you now, believing you have been my mistress.''

Anne felt that his words were insulting and was tempted to tell him of Lord Millbank's offer but refrained. She could not cheapen Lord Millbank's honest offer by using it to taunt Lord Stanton.

''I do not care,'' she repeated. ''I have no desire ever to marry.''

Lord Stanton looked for a moment as though he would say more, but did not. Anne remained standing before her chair, her back stiff with pride and her head held high. Lord Stanton bowed rigidly and took his leave without another word.

Anne sat down slowly, wondering if she had done the right thing. There was a time, that night at Lady Brookfield's, that she had thought to have any of him was better than none. But now she felt the opposite. If she were to marry him without his love and then he took a mistress, she would not have been able to bear it. It would be better to have none of him than to share him.

She attempted to work on her list again, but found that the confrontation with Lord Stanton had shattered her ability to concentrate. She decided to find Melissa. Perhaps some of Melissa's joy would take her mind off her own unhappiness.

AFTER LEAVING ANNE'S HOUSE, Lord Stanton instructed his groom to take the curricle back, and walked home, hoping to walk off some of his anger. Anne Southwell had refused him. He, the Marquess of Talford, owner of a fortune and Longworth, a sought-after catch for over twenty years, had been refused by a disgraced spinster from a country village. It was unthinkable. Arriving at his town house, he thrust his hat and stick at his butler and gave the order for a bottle of claret to be taken to the library.

When Jessup came with the bottle, he instructed that he was not to be disturbed under any circumstances for the rest of the day. He slouched down into his favourite chair, a full glass of claret in his hand. Not until he had heard the stories about her last night had he realized the depth of his feelings for Anne. He had determined then to offer for her and had gone to do so as soon as he could this morning. He'd been nervous but confident. He'd not expected a refusal. He'd thought she might demur but agree in the end that it was the only thing to be done. Then, safely married, he could have wooed her and won her love. He knew she felt a strong physical attraction for him, and that would have been a good start. But she had refused. Why? It could only be that, despite her physical attraction to him, she found him repugnant because of his reputation. He was trying to think of any other possible reasons when his butler entered the room.

"What's this, Jessup? I gave orders that I was not to be disturbed."

"Please, your lordship," explained Jessup. "There is a gentleman below, a Captain Leslie, who refuses to leave and says he will wait as long as necessary to speak with you."

Captain Leslie, thought Lord Stanton, that was the army officer always hanging about Anne. No doubt he had come to issue him a challenge. Well, he couldn't fault him for that.

"Very well, let him come up."

Jessup returned shortly, followed by Captain Leslie, who stood stiffly before Lord Stanton's chair. Lord Stanton did not rise.

"Have you come to call me out, Captain?" he said. "Before you do that I should tell you that I offered for her this morning and she turned me down. Surely honour has been satisfied?"

Captain Leslie did not pretend not to understand who "she" was.

"I see. Then I have come upon a useless errand."

"No, Captain, I respect you for your care of Miss Southwell's name. Although I would like to know by what right you take the defence of Miss Southwell's reputation upon yourself," he said, straightening in his chair, a glower upon his face.

"The right of any gentleman who hears the name of a lady maligned."

"Quite right," Lord Stanton answered, falling back into his chair. Captain Leslie came to defend Anne as a gentleman, not as her betrothed. "Don't worry. She will come about somehow and do quite well without us both, I have no doubt." He looked at Captain Leslie perceptively. "It seems we have something in common. Join me in a drink?"

Captain Leslie viewed Lord Stanton with a mixture of pity and envy. His guess as to who the "other" who held Anne's affections was had evidently been correct. He wondered why she had refused him. "No, thank you, my lord," he said, turning to leave. "My errand is finished."

Lord Stanton looked after Captain Leslie, feeling fractionally better. It was obvious Anne had not accepted the captain's hand, either. But what were her reasons? Did she truly not desire ever to marry? He was mulling over the problem when the door opened again.

"Damn it, I said I was not to be disturbed, Jessup."

"Jessup knows better than to try and refuse me," answered his sister, coming in and closing the door behind her. She stood before him in the place recently occupied by Captain Leslie, looking down at him disapprovingly. "It is time you told me everything."

Lord Stanton did not argue, but wearily motioned for her to be seated. Fortifying himself with another drink, he told her the whole, including his offer that morning and Anne's rejection of it. Lady Brookfield listened in astonishment, then with growing satisfaction. She could see, if her brother could not, that Miss Southwell had a deep feeling for him.

"Go ahead, ring a peal over me and then leave," he said ungraciously as he finished his recital.

"It would appear there is no need. Although I am appalled that even you would enter upon such a reprehensive wager with an unmarried woman of gentle blood," she added, unable to resist giving her brother a mild dressing-down. "But it is obvious you are not in a condition to benefit from my advice."

Her scolding was interrupted by the arrival of Jessup. Lord Stanton raised his eyebrows sardonically.

"I *am* losing my touch. A woman refuses my hand, and now my servants don't obey me."

"It's from the Prince, your lordship," explained Jessup, holding out a silver salver with a note upon it.

Lord Stanton opened it resignedly. "Prinny is commanding my immediate attendance at Carlton House. I suppose I must go. Excuse me, Caroline," he said, pushing himself up from his chair. "Jessup, find Lewis and have him come try to make something of my attire."

"I WAS MOST DISPLEASED to hear the *on dit*s about Miss Southwell and Miss Amberly, Stanton," reproved the Prince of Wales, a severe expression upon his face.

Lord Stanton knew from the fact that he was left standing in the Prince's presence and that he was not offered refreshment that Prinny was most displeased with him.

"You will make an offer to Miss Southwell immediately," the Prince commanded.

"I already did so, sir," Lord Stanton replied. "She refused me."

"Refused you, eh?" The Prince looked surprised. Stanton was generally considered a good catch, despite his reputation.

"Refused me. Not even to save her own reputation would Miss Southwell contemplate an alliance with 'Hell-born Harry,'" he finished bitterly.

The prince looked at Lord Stanton with sudden understanding.

"So that's it. Sit down, Stanton," he said, motioning to a chair, his geniality returning.

Lord Stanton sat. The Prince offered him a cherry brandy and looked at him thoughtfully. The personal interest Prince George took in the problems of his friends was one of his most attractive qualities.

"You have obviously botched it, Stanton. Leave it to me. You don't know how to handle women, at least not respectable ones."

"There is nothing to be done. She was quite adamant in her refusal."

"Leave it me," the Prince repeated.

Lord Stanton made no more protests, but he doubted very much the Prince would be able to help, however good his intentions. There were limits, even to what a Prince could achieve.

CHAPTER TWELVE

AFTER THE FIRST difficult day when Lord Stanton had made his ungracious offer, Anne was surprised to see how little their ostracism by the haut ton upset her life, although its effects were evident. Even the appearance of the announcement of the engagement between Melissa and Lieutenant Halcott in the *Gazette* did not lead to an increase in their invitations to social functions. Anne did not miss the constant round of entertainments, and Melissa claimed she did not miss them either, immersed as she was in the plans for her wedding. They did go occasionally to Drury Lane and Covent Garden in the company of the Halcotts, but only the Millbanks and Brookfields came to their box between acts.

Lady Amelia seemed the most distressed by their ostracism, missing her best friend's company at the various entertainments. Her friendship with Melissa had given her more self-confidence, and she felt the want of her support.

"It is so unfair," Lady Amelia declared one morning. "No one will listen to the truth of what really happened. Even Mama was not going to allow me to call upon you anymore, but George told her that we would, whatever she said, and reminded her that *he* is the head of the family," she said, looking at her brother proudly.

Lord Millbank appeared embarrassed at his sister's words, and busied himself taking a pinch of snuff from a new cobalt-blue snuffbox.

"But I must tell you my news," Lady Amelia continued. She looked shyly at Melissa. "Lord Woolbridge has asked George for permission to pay his addresses."

Melissa hugged her friend joyfully, and Anne gave her best wishes. She and Melissa had been correct in their assessment of the situation. Lord Woolbridge had come to appreciate the quiet qualities of Lady Amelia. Lord Millbank looked proudly at his younger sister, pleased that she had captured such an eligible party. Anne felt her load of guilt lighten a little more. Another person whom she had feared had been hurt by her irresponsible behaviour was once again happy.

Lady Amelia pressed Melissa and her guardian to attend the ball at which her betrothal would be announced, but they reluctantly refused, begging her to understand.

"I understand," Lady Amelia said, "but I did so wish you to be present, Melissa." She sighed. "At least when we are both married we will be able to receive each other."

Taking comfort in that hope, they pledged to attend each other's weddings, and Lord Millbank and Lady Amelia took their leave.

THAT NIGHT ANNE AND MELISSA were engaged to attend one of the few functions still open to them—a supper party at the Halcotts'. Mrs. Halcott had been careful to invite no one who did not fully support her protégées, and the evening passed more pleasantly than Anne had expected. She was reminded of their first supper there, even to being seated next to Captain Leslie. It had only been a few months ago, but their lives had changed so since that it seemed years.

When the gentlemen rejoined the women after their port, Mrs. Halcott asked Anne to entertain the company by playing a piece upon the pianoforte. She agreed, and played a sprightly sonata by Mozart. Then her place at the pianoforte was taken by Melissa, who accompanied herself to several light airs. As Anne sat listening to her, she was approached by Captain Leslie.

"Miss Southwell, would you join me on a walk in the garden?" he asked quietly.

Anne agreed, surprised, for Captain Leslie had avoided being alone in her presence since the day she had told him she loved another. She rose, and they left the drawing room together unobtrusively.

The Halcotts' garden was small, but pleasant, and they walked to a stone bench, where, by mutual consent, they stopped and sat together. For a few moments they sat quietly, enjoying the strong evening fragrance of the flowers. Then Captain Leslie broke the silence.

"I wish to tell you that I shall be leaving London. I have a few weeks leave, and I shall be going to Brighton ahead of my regiment."

Anne felt a great sense of loss. She and Captain Leslie no longer enjoyed the free and easy comradeship they had shared before, but there was still a bond between them. Anne knew that he had been deeply hurt by her refusal of him, and realized that the move was probably the best thing; however, she would miss him.

"I will be sorry to see you go," she said, looking at him sadly, knowing it might be the last time she saw him. He sat next to her, erect in his dark green Rifles uniform, the gold trim matching the gold of his hair as it shone in the moonlight. His blue eyes reflected a sorrow that had not been there previously.

"Remember," he said sincerely, "if you are ever in need, a note to the 12th Rifles will bring me to your aid."

Overcome, Anne took his hand and pressed it between hers. Captain Leslie bent forward and kissed her softly on the lips. They sat hand in hand a long while before they rose and walked slowly back to the house, knowing that this was farewell.

THE NEXT MORNING, Anne had trouble shaking off the sense of sadness brought about by Captain Leslie's departure. She was working on the guest list for Melissa's wedding when Benton brought an invitation to her, holding out the silver salver with a flourish. Anne was surprised to recognize a thick gold-edged invitation from Carlton House.

She opened it with a heavy heart. It must be the influence of Lord Stanton again. Did he think that another invitation to Carlton House would once more reinstate them? Didn't he realize that they were beyond redeeming in the eyes of Society? They were more likely to think she was one of the Prince's mistresses, she reflected.

She glanced over the invitation, having no intention of going, when she noticed some differences in this one from her first. It stated that a carriage would be sent for her and seemed to be signed by the Prince of Wales himself, instead of his secretary. She sighed, supposing she would have to go. It appeared to be a royal command. She looked at the invitation again. It said she would be picked up at half past seven on the fourteenth—three days from now. Melissa was not included. Perhaps the Prince *was* intending to make her his mistress, she thought wryly. In any case, she could not refuse a royal summons.

Anne showed Melissa the invitation, who was as puzzled by it as Anne, but agreed that she must go, as did Mrs. Halcott when she was informed. Privately,

Mrs. Halcott also feared that the Prince was planning to make Anne his mistress. She told Anne to avoid being alone with him, and that if she got into an uncomfortable situation to put him off by telling him she had a chill. The Prince's fear of contagion was well known.

That Thursday Anne dressed as elegantly as she could. If she were going to be thought a Fashionable Impure she might as well look like one. She chose her most elaborate gown, a trained robe of gold edged in trim of the Greek key design. It opened in the front to expose a petticoat of white satin heavily embroidered in gold thread and overlaid with gold net. She wore her headdress of ostrich feathers, and since it would be bad manners to appear at Carlton House without jewellery, she again borrowed Mrs. Halcott's diamonds. When the carriage picked her up, complete with the royal insignia on the door, she knew that the neighbours would be thinking the worst.

The driver did not take her to the front entrance of Carlton House as she had expected, but to the back. Here she was met by a servant in blue-and-gold livery who led her into the palace and directly to the room where the supper was being held. Most of the guests were already seated. Her idea that the Prince intended to make her his mistress gained in strength when she was conducted to the table where Prinny himself sat. The servant guided her to her place, where, to her anger and horror, she was seated between Lord Stanton and Beau Brummel. She could not imagine two people she would less have liked to be next to. She had not seen or spoken to Lord Stanton since the day of his ungracious proposal, and Brummel she had assiduously avoided the entire Season, fearing his cruel tongue might damage her ward's chances if he chose to direct it against her.

She sat stiffly between them, looking at neither. When the guests were all seated, Anne barely noticed when the Prince rose from the table and addressed the company.

"My friends," he said graciously, "I am holding this small supper party in honour of the betrothal of a close friend of mine. I am pleased to announce the engagement of Henry Stanton, Marquess of Talford, to Miss Southwell, daughter of Major Southwell." He smiled benignly and raised his glass in their direction.

Anne went into shock at the Prince's words. Lord Stanton had arranged this somehow. How *dared* he! He knew she could not refute the Prince. She sat immobile, staring at the Prince, her eyes wide, until she felt a hand under her elbow forcing her to rise. Lord Stanton, seemingly fully in control, bowed to the Prince and thanked him gracefully. Prinny, beaming, sat down and began helping himself to the dishes before him. The rest of the guests followed suit.

Anne, still in shock, sat rigidly, unable to speak or eat. Gradually, a voice next to her impinged upon her consciousness.

"Miss Southwell," it was saying, "may I serve you some poached turbot? I recommend it highly." Mr. Brummel, for it was he speaking, placed a small amount upon her plate.

With a tremendous act of will, Anne forced herself to gain control. She must eat—she sat directly under the Prince's eye. She could not offend him, and could not attract adverse attention by sitting frozen at her place all evening. She thanked the Beau and began to eat, although the fish tasted like ashes in her mouth.

As the meal went on, she became grateful for the fact that Mr. Brummel sat next to her. He spoke to her easily, not appearing to notice anything out of the way in her short and sometimes irrelevant answers to his questions. She paid no attention to Lord Stanton on her left, and he in turn occupied himself talking to the woman on his other side. Perversely, this angered Anne, and only the impeccable social graces of the Beau helped her to get through the interminable supper without error.

At last the Prince rose from the table, and Anne felt a hand under her elbow again, forcing her to rise also. As they worked their way through the room, many of the company came to offer congratulations, and Lord Stanton answered them easily. Anne pasted a frozen smile upon her face and only nodded in response to remarks addressed to her. Slowly and surely Lord Stanton manoeuvred her through the crowded rooms, acknowledging the wishes of his friends. He seemed to know his way around, and was soon able to slip with her into an empty passageway. He led her unprotestingly down the hall and into a small salon illuminated by a blazing fire. He shut the door and leaned against it. At last Anne came out of her trance.

"How dare you!" she raved at Lord Stanton, turning to face him angrily. "You knew I could not refute what the Prince said. How dare you!"

"I had nothing to do with it. It was as much a shock to me as it was to you," Lord Stanton said grimly. "It was Prinny's idea entirely. I had no inkling of his plans until you were seated beside me."

"You expect me to believe that?" Anne cried. "I told you it was not necessary for you to sacrifice yourself to save my reputation. Melissa is marrying Lieutenant Halcott, and I intend to return to Medford. I no longer care what Society says of me."

"Will you listen to me," Lord Stanton said in frustration. "I tell you I had nothing to do with this."

Anne, furious at the realization that she would now be forced to marry Lord Stanton and live with him knowing he did not care for her, continued to storm at him wildly.

Finally, Lord Stanton lost patience. "By gad, I think Prinny may have the right of it in his lessons to me on how to woo a woman," he swore. He grabbed Anne, pinning her arms to her side, and began to kiss her roughly.

Anne, frightened lest her true feelings for Lord Stanton show, fought to be free from his embrace, but he only held her more tightly. He forced her backwards and onto a low sofa against the wall, his lips continuing to plunder hers. His weight pushed her down until they were half reclining together on the sofa, his arms still around her. Her resistance weakened at the nearness and touch of the man she loved so much, and finally crumbled. Tentatively, she moved her lips beneath his.

Lord Stanton, feeling the difference in her response, raised his face from hers and looked at her intently. Anne knew her love was there for him to see, but she no longer cared. Her pride had gone. "Anne," he said softly, touching her face softly. She caught his fingers in her hand and held them lightly, a gentle gesture that seemed to inflame Lord Stanton. He crushed her against his body and began to kiss her demandingly. Anne returned his kisses willingly, drowning in an ocean of new sensations. Then, as from a far distance, she heard a groan from Lord Stanton, and he pulled away from her, sitting up and taking her hand in his. Anne, confused and embarrassed by the passion she had displayed, sat up, too, keeping her eyes downcast and half-shut.

"Anne," Lord Stanton said softly, leaning forward and caressing her hair with his free hand.

Anne's heavy-lidded eyes opened fractionally. "Yes?"

"Why did you refuse me that morning?"

Anne hesitated, unsure whether to confess her love for him or not. He had displayed desire for her, and tenderness, but he had not said he loved her. "It was your manner," she said. "You were so cold—I did not want you to marry me because you felt you had to, and then resent me for the rest of your life."

"So that was it," he chuckled, "and I thought it was because I was 'Hell-born Harry,' a disreputable rake that no respectable woman would have if she did not desire my fortune or my title, which you obviously did not."

"How could I object to you on those grounds when I am not received by most of the ton myself?" Anne asked. "But why were you so cold?"

"I wasn't cold; I was nervous," Lord Stanton admitted. "I had come to realise only the night before how deeply I loved you, and I was not sure it was something you would want to hear. Then, after your refusal," he further confessed, "I was angry."

Anne responded only to the first of his comments. "Not want to hear!" she repeated. "There was nothing more in the world I wished to hear than that you loved me," she said her eyes fully open now.

Lord Stanton looked into their green depths and drew her towards him, holding her close.

"Well," he said after a moment, "are you going to confess you love me, too, or do my instincts tell me wrong?"

"Oh, yes, Lord Stanton, I love you with all my heart," she said, the truth of the statement evident in her eyes.

"'Harry,' my dear. I think 'Lord Stanton' is a little formal."

Anne laughed, relaxing into his arms and leaning her golden head against his shoulder. She felt comfortable there, secure in his love and strength. Who would have thought, the day she made the wager, that this would be the result? Remembering the wager caused a new thought to occur to her, and a small sound of distress escaped her throat.

"What is it, my dear?" Lord Stanton asked with concern, looking down into her suddenly troubled face.

Anne blushed, unsure whether to put what had occurred to her in words. "I've just realised that I did not pay my wager. I know you released me from it, but you shouldn't have. What happened was only what you warned me about in the beginning. It doesn't feel right, not keeping my obligations. What would Charlie have said?"

Lord Stanton laughed richly and tipped Anne's head up so she was looking directly at him. "I have every intention of collecting the wager—after we're married."

WHEN LORD STANTON HANDED ANNE from his carriage before her house on Half Moon Street, they were surprised to see that the residence was still brightly lit. Melissa had evidently waited up for her return.

Lord Stanton accompanied Anne inside, and they went up to the drawing room together, Benton looking after them uncertainly. Melissa got up from the chair where she had been working on some embroidery, a look of shock on her face at seeing Anne in the company of Lord Stanton.

"It's all right, Melissa," Anne reassured her, "Lord Stanton and I are betrothed."

"Betrothed?" Melissa repeated, looking at them dubiously. "Do you *wish* to be?"

Lord Stanton laughed. "I know it is unbelievable that a respectable woman should agree to marry a disreputable person like myself, but I assure you, it is so."

"Not so respectable," Sanders muttered from the corner where she sat with some sewing. "It took you long enough," she added more loudly. "You should have offered for her last January after that first evening. Drinking brandy alone with an unmarried woman with the door closed." She shook her head disgustedly. "But I suppose it's better late than never."

Lord Stanton grinned. "I agree."

THREE MONTHS LATER the Marquess and Marchioness of Talford, in residence at their estate of Longworth for the summer, inspected a large parcel that had arrived from London.

"It's a gift from Prinny," said Lord Stanton, reading the card he had been handed by the messenger. "A wedding gift."

"I believe it is a painting," said Anne, watching curiously as the footman endeavoured to undo it.

Suddenly Lord Stanton began to laugh. "What would you wager, my dear, that it is a Fragonard?"

"Wager, my love?" Anne said innocently. "I have no need of wagers now, and I belive, sir, you have been paid in full."

"And with great interest I might add," he said with a wicked grin.

They laughed together as they stood back to admire the gilt-framed painting revealed. With their arms about each other they surveyed the three robust but attractive nudes in a muted forest setting. It was a Rubens, not a Fragonard.

"What do you think?" asked Lord Stanton, his arm tightening about his wife's waist. "He remembered the story I told him of our first meeting."

"I think," said Anne, turning in her husband's arms and placing a kiss upon his lips, ignoring the presence of the footman, "that it should hang in a place of honour in the Long Gallery."

Harlequin Regency Romance™

COMING NEXT MONTH

#19 LUCINDA by Blanche Chenier

Lucinda Edrington is down at the heels and must sell her family home to pay her brother's debts. Her new neighbour, Lord Sarne, would like to help, but is constantly attended by a woman with designs on him. In an effort to keep Lucinda and Lord Sarne apart, a rumour is circulated that Lucinda was born on the wrong side of the blanket. Lord Sarne, however, sees through the deception and rescues Lucinda from her various misadventures just in time to propose a marriage she never dreamed possible.

#20 THE VICAR'S DAUGHTER by Eva Rutland

With her father so ill, Christina Frame appeals to the Earl of Wakefield to finance his recovery in Spain. The earl agrees to do so if Christina will marry his profligate son, Domenic Winston, Viscount Stanhope. Christina and Domenic agree for reasons of their own. While Domenic intends to pursue the freedom that marriage allows, he soon finds himself too busy to do so. So busy is he that he does not realize that he has fallen in love with the wife he had tried so hard to avoid until it is almost too late.